Don't do this, he told himself. ***Stop it***

Not that any relevant part of him was listening.

Dixie was gazing up at him, the moonlight reflecting in her blue, blue eyes. He longed to run his hands through her sweet-smelling hair, press his body close to hers and whisper softly in her ear.

She saw his intent and she did not back away. Even though he'd known her only a bit longer than twenty-four hours, even though when they'd met he'd been wearing a Yankee uniform.

"Oh, Kyle," she said, exhaling his name on a long breath. Before she could tell him to stop, he did what was possibly the stupidest thing in his life, considering that he quite possibly still had a girlfriend back in Ohio.

He swept her up his arms and kissed her....

Dear Reader,

I recently attended a Civil War reenactment near Charleston, South Carolina, and found myself caught up in that long-ago time. The costumes, the encampment and the battle itself made me stop and think about my ancestors who were around during The Late Great Unpleasantness, as we Southerners still refer to it.

I wondered how many of the present-day soldiers on the battlefield were descendants of men who fought in that war and if any of them were related to me. Why did these men become reenactors, anyway? Why didn't they want to forget that awful conflict that took such a toll upon both the Union and the Confederacy? As I seriously considered these questions, my hero, Kyle Tecumseh Sherman, took shape in my imagination. He appeared full-grown, a descendant of the Union general William Tecumseh Sherman. He even looked like him! I knew right away that Kyle would be dedicated to preserving the memory of all who fought in that war, North and South.

I'd already created a heroine who was made to order for Kyle. She's Dixie Lee Smith, sister of Carolina Rose Smith in my book *Down Home Carolina Christmas*. Dixie was named for both the lost Confederacy and the South's most revered general, Robert E. Lee. It was inevitable that when Dixie Lee Smith and Kyle Tecumseh Sherman met, sparks would fly.

And they did—all kinds of sparks, including the kind that light a fire too hot to quench, a fire that I hope will warm your heart as it does mine.

With love and best wishes,

Pamela Browning

Down Home Dixie
PAMELA BROWNING

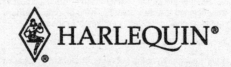

HARLEQUIN®

TORONTO • NEW YORK • LONDON
AMSTERDAM • PARIS • SYDNEY • HAMBURG
STOCKHOLM • ATHENS • TOKYO • MILAN • MADRID
PRAGUE • WARSAW • BUDAPEST • AUCKLAND

ISBN-13: 978-0-373-75212-6
ISBN-10:   0-373-75212-1

DOWN HOME DIXIE

This edition published by arrangement with Harlequin Books S.A.

® and TM are trademarks of the publisher. Trademarks indicated with ® are registered in the United States Patent and Trademark Office, the Canadian Trade Marks Office and in other countries.

www.eHarlequin.com

Printed in U.S.A.

ABOUT THE AUTHOR

Pamela Browning spent a lot of years living and rearing a family in a charming South Carolina town that was nothing like Yewville. No one in this book bears any resemblance whatever to persons living, dead or comatose, except for Muffin the cat, who will never reveal her real name. Never. *If* she wants her catnip mouse refilled on a regular basis.

Pamela enjoys hearing from her readers and invites you to visit her Web site at www.pamelabrowning.com

Books by Pamela Browning

HARLEQUIN AMERICAN ROMANCE

This book is dedicated to battle reenactors
and the people who support them.
They keep history brilliantly alive for all of us.

Chapter One

You wouldn't expect to find a confused and disoriented Union soldier rambling around the parking lot of the dentist's office, but that's exactly what Dixie Lee Smith saw in the dwindling hours of a beautiful spring Saturday afternoon in Yewville, South Carolina.

As she slid behind the wheel of her car, she noted that he was tall. He was handsome. He was uncommonly pale, even for a Yankee.

She turned on the car engine. And then she shot him.

Looking incredulous, he braced his back against the trunk of a nearby oak tree, and slid slowly to a sitting position on the ground. A dark stain—blood?—marked his upper left chest beside the toothbrush sticking out of his pocket. The toothbrush bore the dentist's logo: Gregory Johnson, D.D.S., Yewville, SC.

How could she have shot the man? She didn't even have a gun. Still, there had been a terribly loud bang, and no one else was around. Horrified, she scrambled out of her car.

"Are you in pain?"

"No. And yes. It's not what you think," the man said, using the tree trunk to pull himself up.

"What do I think?" Dixie said, not quite believing she'd asked such a stupid question. Her excuse for her own present befuddlement was that she'd been pumped full of lidocaine after being talked into two fillings when all she wanted was her teeth whitened. It tended to numb her all over, lidocaine did.

"I only lost my balance," the soldier said. He cupped a hand around his jaw as if it hurt. "Well, I *was* shot, but not really. Don't worry about it. That noise scared me, that's all."

He must be joking, she thought, taking in the elaborate epaulets and dashing sleeve insignia on the blue uniform. *He's not making sense.* On the other hand, she probably wasn't, either.

Uppermost in Dixie's mind was that when some years ago her father had been administered morphine for postoperative pain, he was certain he'd spotted Senator Strom Thurmond attired in a Batman outfit reclining on a cloud outside his hospital window. He'd insisted the senator had been eating a chocolate banana on a stick like the ones they sold at the Southern Confectionery Kitchen right here in Yewville. It had taken a heap of talking to persuade Daddy that Strom Thurmond was still in Washington and not hitching rides on stratocumulus Batmobiles.

So maybe this was the same kind of thing. However, did hallucinations go to the dentist? And concentrate on their jaws when they'd been shot in the chest? He said he *hadn't* been shot. Or did he say he *had?* Dixie was growing even more confused.

The man lurched on wobbly legs toward a vehicle that appeared to be a cross between an ice-cream truck and the local coroner's van. He dug his car keys out of his pocket.

"Your car backfired," he mumbled. "You'd better get it checked."

Well, that would explain the loud bang. She'd had the Mustang's carburetor adjusted yesterday.

"Shouldn't you see a doctor? For that chest wound of yours? There's a hospital here, eighty-eight beds and a good emergency room."

The man regarded her balefully. "I need a motel where I can stay for the night. I'm not really hurt. I'm a Civil War battle reenactor, and the blood is fake."

Okay. How was I to know? "The Magnolia Motel's out on the bypass. They should be able to fix you up with a room."

"I checked there on my way into town. They're full up."

"Oh, must be another tour bus. Lately the Magnolia never has vacancies on weekends." The fact that the town water tower was painted like a giant peach but more closely resembled a fuzzy pink derriere had something to do with the recent increase of tourism in these parts.

"Are there any other hotels in town? I'm desperate."

She'd like to help him out, but that uniform turned her off, as it would any respectable Southerner even so long after what was still referred to around here as the War of Northern Aggression. Or as he called it, the Civil War, though Dixie was quite sure that there had been nothing civil about it.

While Dixie tried to figure out what to do, the Yankee dropped his keys. Right at her feet. And bent over in an attempt to retrieve them only to straighten in pain, giving a little moan.

She picked up the keys. It seemed the polite thing, and besides, she hated to see anyone in pain.

"I'd better not drive," he said unsteadily. "Is there a taxi service?"

"I wish."

"A boardinghouse? Anything?"

She tried to think. "The only boardinghouse closed when the last Pankey sister died."

"I could sleep in the back of my truck. I have a sleeping bag," he said.

"Our local police chief tends to hustle vagrants out of town real fast."

The soldier leaned against his truck and closed his eyes. They were several lovely shades of golden brown, putting her in mind of autumn leaves floating on the tea-colored water of Sycamore Branch. His hair, at least what she could see of it peeking out from under the cap, was a gingery color, or maybe chestnut depending on the amount of light glinting through the trees. He was a handsome guy if you didn't mind the sharpness of his nose.

Dixie wondered at the wisdom of getting involved in this situation.

"Look, uh, sir," she said. "I could ask my friend Bubba if you can stay in his spare room."

"Anything," the soldier said. "Anything at all."

He recognized her indecision for what it was and looked her straight in the eye. "I promise I'm harmless, and I've never been in trouble with the law," he said, adding, "except for a parking ticket when I was seventeen."

Dixie whipped out her cell phone. "Bubba, would you consider renting your spare room for the night?" Bubba had recently married, but before that, he'd endured a succession of boarders in the second bedroom of his small brick house.

"You got to be kidding," Bubba said. A television set provided background roars, which let Dixie know that Bubba was watching a NASCAR race on TV.

"I'm not joking," Dixie said with the utmost seriousness. "I have a man in need here, and the Magnolia Motel is full."

"Listen, Dixie, I always like to help someone out, but my old coon dog and her new puppies are occupying the spare bedroom at present." A pause. "Hey, did you hear that?"

"I maybe heard a tire blowing out."

"That was no tire. That was the caps popping off the beer I made."

"You make beer now? Is that legal?"

"As long as it's for my own consumption."

Dixie opened her mouth to ask why the bottle caps were popping, but Bubba was back to business. "Sorry, Dixie, but I really can't take on a guest right now. My bride wouldn't take kindly to the intrusion. Katie's pregnant, in case you haven't heard."

"Yes, she told me. Congratulations," Dixie said, but Bubba and Katie's news hit hard. With so many of her friends already married and having babies, Dixie was convinced that life was passing her by. She deserved a husband. She deserved a family. But when was it going to happen for her? Soon, if she had anything to say about it. That's why she'd embarked on a self-improvement program that included teeth whitening.

"Well," she said to the Yankee after she clicked off, "that didn't work out." *To say the least.*

"I'm sorry to be so much trouble," the soldier said apologetically. "I have an overblown reaction to anesthetics sometimes. Since Dr. Johnson isn't my regular dentist, I suspect he gave me more than I can handle." He spoke with a Midwestern accent, certainly not Southern. Which, Dixie supposed, was to be expected. No self-respecting Southern man would ever entertain wearing that uniform, reenactor or not.

Still, he was counting on her, and Dixie wasn't prepared to give up. "Just one more phone call, okay? This one in private."

The soldier only stared.

"Are you going to be all right standing there?" she asked him.

"Maybe not. I'm going to sit down on that bench." He navigated sideways to a white wrought iron bench situated beside a forsythia bush in full bloom.

She waited until he sat and cautioned, "You'd better drop your head between your legs. You look a bit puny."

He seemed as if he'd pass out any moment. She steadied him by holding his arm, figuring that even if he was Jack the Ripper, he was in no condition to do her any harm. After a time, he lifted his head. "Wow," he said wonderingly. "I felt as if I was going to faint."

She released his arm as soon as he rallied but not before noting the firm bulge of muscle beneath the blue fabric. She hadn't wrapped her hands around a muscle like that since the local National Guard unit shipped out to the Middle East. It occurred to her that she wouldn't mind feeling this one again under the right circumstances.

"Like I said, I need to make another call," she told him before hurrying to her car. Keeping a watchful eye on the Yankee, who continued to sit hunched on the hard bench with his elbows balanced on his knees, she dialed her friend Jasper Beasley, Yewville police chief, and recited the number on the truck's Ohio license tag.

"I'll run the tag, see what I can find," Jasper promised, not even asking her why she needed the information. Dixie and Jasper went all the way back to the first day of kindergarten when he'd smashed her flat in the school yard at recess and then picked her up, dusted her off and offered her a moon pie. They'd remained good friends.

Dixie waited in the car, observing the Yankee from a safe

distance. Those uniform sleeves were a bit short, exposing thick wrists and large meaty hands. He had a mole on his left cheek, kind of sexy. His hair tended to curl at the back of his neck, and she wished he'd take off that danged cap so she could study the shape of his head. Her grandmother's belief was that you could divine a lot about a man from the shape of his head; a high forehead meant an intellectual bent, a rounded curve at the back of the crown meant more room for a brain to develop, and a pointy head—well, Memaw Frances always cautioned not to get involved with one of those.

Her phone played the crazy *ka-ching ka-ching* cash-register ring that she'd chosen after starting to work full-time as a real estate agent.

"Dixie, that license tag comes up clean," Jasper told her. "The vehicle is registered to Kyle T. Sherman of Ledbetter, Ohio, a suburb of Columbus. No priors, no record of any kind."

"All right," she said, eyeing the Yankee. He didn't seem like a Kyle. He looked more like a Brian to her, or a Scott, but he wasn't responsible for the name his parents gave him any more than she was for being named Dixie Lee. Kyle was a decent name, hunky but not overbearing, trendy without being funky.

"Anything else I can do for you?" Jasper asked.

"No, that's all for now. Thanks, Jasper. Tell Lori I said hi."

"Sure will. When you coming over for dinner again?"

"Next time Lori makes Brunswick stew," she told him.

"She'll call you. I got to shoot a mess of squirrels first."

They hung up, and Dixie slid out of the car.

At her approach, the Yankee lifted his head as though he'd been run over by a tractor. The only thing he lacked was tread marks.

"Come on," Dixie said brusquely. "I'm taking you home with me."

"Don't wanna be any trouble," he said. "I'm a little wobbly at the moment, that's all."

"You can sleep in my cottage," she said, not adding that it had once been a child's playhouse. She'd stored plant containers there with the intention of using the building for a potting shed, but right now it could provide shelter.

"Is it all right to leave my truck here?"

"Doc Johnson probably won't mind."

"My name's Kyle Sherman," the soldier said after he folded himself into the passenger side of the Mustang. "I can't tell you how grateful I am."

"No problem," she assured him, though she had her misgivings. It was ingrained in her to be hospitable to strangers. She couldn't imagine walking away and leaving him sitting outside the dentist's office when he had no place to stay.

"You haven't told me your name," he reminded her.

"Dixie Lee Smith," she said without elaborating. She could have told him that she'd lived in Yewville all her life, that her house was only ten minutes outside of town, that she'd bought it as a fixer-upper and moved in less than a week ago. She aimed a covert glance at the Yankee. His jaw was solid, and if Memaw's theories held true, this bespoke a strong character. He had square teeth that put her in mind of an advertisement for Chiclets, and his ears, though partly hidden beneath the cap, were rather large. He was cleanly shaven, which was all to the good, since she'd never been partial to facial hair. She believed that sometimes men who grew a mustache or a beard had something to hide, like a short upper lip or a weak chin. That was not the case with Kyle Sherman.

An odd thought occurred to her, but she brushed it away. Sherman was not a respected name around here, considering that General William Tecumseh Sherman's men had swept through South Carolina in 1864, burning the state capital only seventy miles away and pillaging Yewville and other small towns after their famous march to the sea.

She hoped this reenactor was not related to *that* Sherman. Lordy, if he was, and if the ladies of the local chapter of the United Daughters of the Confederacy ever found out she was assisting him, she could forget about joining the chapter, even though her grandmother was one of its most respected members.

"Uh-oh, I'm going to be sick," Kyle said. His face had gone a peculiar shade of green.

She pulled over, lurching onto the shoulder of the road just in time for him to wrench open the door and upchuck into a tangle of briars.

He leaned back into the car. "Sorry," he said.

Wordlessly she handed him a bottle of water from the cache she kept on the back seat. He drank, wiped his face with a handkerchief and inhaled a deep breath.

"I swear, I've never felt so awful," he said. "Is it far to your place?"

Embarrassed for him, she shook her head. "Just a few more minutes."

As he slumped back into his corner, Dixie eased the Mustang back onto the road and mashed hard on the accelerator, not caring in the least if she exceeded the speed limit.

"Do you always drive this fast?" he asked.

"When someone in my car is sick, yes."

He didn't comment, and she reached home in record time. She braked to a stop beside the old playhouse.

Kyle got out of the car before she asked if she could help him. "The fresh air clears my head," he explained, inhaling deeply several times.

"How's your stomach?" she asked.

"Better now." He'd regained some color, and he sounded stronger.

"Follow me."

The playhouse had been there for years, the children who had once enjoyed it long gone. The path was overgrown with encroaching azalea bushes, the rough-hewn arched door almost obscured by drooping vines. Her guest had to duck his head and shoulders to enter.

The structure was a one-room affair with a cramped bathroom. A real kitchen ranged along one wall, though everything in it was only three-quarter size, and a narrow cot was squeezed into the space under a round window.

"A Hobbit house?" Kyle mused as she shoved aside several flowerpots and a bag of potting soil.

"Not quite," she said, though the description was apt. "At least it's a place to sleep. I'll run over to the house and bring back sheets and pillows."

While she was speaking, he inspected the cot and lifted the quilt. "It already has sheets," he declared. He sat down heavily, making the springs squeak and releasing a slightly musty odor. "I'm still pretty weak," he offered in explanation.

She'd figured that out for herself. "Be right back," she told him.

Since she'd just moved in, she wasn't nearly settled. Still, her new house never failed to lift her spirits when she approached it. The house had been built haphazardly, one section at a time, which resulted in odd doors, unplanned niches and dormers inserted in unlikely places, but the result was pleasant. The back door opened into the kitchen. Beyond it was a hall leading to a sewing room and the front-door foyer. The adjacent living room was still piled high with boxes. Upstairs were three bedrooms. The house was too big for her. However, the previous owners had been eager to sell for much lower than their asking price and she'd never been one to pass up a bargain.

When she returned with the towels, an ice bag for his swelling jaw and a few other things he might need, Kyle Sherman had tucked himself neatly into bed. The stained Yankee uniform was draped over one of the small chairs, and she had the suspicion that he was naked under the quilt. Certainly his chest, with boldly defined pectorals and a light dusting of dark hair, was impressive, and as far as she could tell, so was the rest of him. He took up most of the width of the cot, which kept her from thinking what it would be like to occupy it beside him.

Where had that idea come from, anyway? She shouldn't be musing about sharing a stranger's bed, but perhaps such startling fantasies were to be expected now that all the eligible men were in the military or deployed with the National Guard or out of work. Ever since Yewville Mills, the town's main industry, had up and moved to Mexico, good men were hard to find.

And hard men were good to find, as Mae West had once said. Dixie pulled herself away from that line of reflection.

"I brought you a few bottles of water," she said briskly as she set them on the table. "And a Thermos of iced tea. It's sweetened, not like you drink it up north. You can share whatever my dinner turns out to be." Her sore gums felt like a pincushion at present and would determine what she could eat. Likely that was his problem, as well.

"Thank you," he said, studying her as if seeing her for the first time. "Like I said, I really appreciate this. I've heard about Southern hospitality, but this is way over the top."

"You'll feel okay by tomorrow," she said. "Your color is better already."

"I'm a lot more comfortable now that I'm lying down."

"That's good," she replied. He didn't have a pointy head, a development that pleased her greatly.

"It was a simple root canal," he said in bewilderment. "I figured I was lucky to find the only dentist in the whole state who keeps office hours on Saturday and who could work me in on short notice. I called him from the battlefield and he said to come on over. So—"

"What battlefield?"

He didn't seem to mind the interruption. "Rivervale Bridge. My unit had a reenactment there this weekend. That's where I got shot. Fake blood to make it more authentic for the audience."

"That's disgusting, making a game out of war."

"Oh, I don't think so."

"I suppose the Union always wins," she said before she could help herself. Immediately, she regretted her snarkiness. But it was too late though to take it back now.

His eyes crinkled when he smiled. "Not at all," he said. "I recently took part in a reenactment at Manassas, Virginia, where Johnny Reb trounced us big-time."

"What happens after these battles? Everybody picks up their guns and goes home?"

"More or less."

"As opposed to the real thing, where a lot of good men died." She couldn't help it. She'd been a participant in too many Confederate Memorial Day ceremonies. Twice, she'd been chosen to lay the wreath on the monument in Memorial Park where the names of several of her forebears were inscribed. And moreover, she'd lost two friends to snipers in Afghanistan, great guys that she would mourn forever. She couldn't comprehend why reenactors liked to play at war.

It took Kyle a few seconds to answer. When he did, his voice was respectful. "Good men were lost on both sides. And that's why we reenactors do what we do—to educate people about the hardships of war, one of which is dying. And to commemorate the men who gave up their lives in the conflict."

His gaze was steady, and she found herself mesmerized by his deep voice. "You see, Dixie, when we reenactors return to where the battle took place, we live the same way as the soldiers who fought. We sleep in tents, shiver in the rain and cook our food over sputtering campfires. We wear the same kind of clothes as they did, constructed out of the same type of fabric. We endure insects and lack of refrigeration. At night, when we miss home and family, we sing their songs. We try to *be* them, for a few days or even a week.

"Even so, we can't *imagine* what it was really like. We're not going to die out there of dysentery or be captured and sent to a prison and we're not going to take a musket ball in the gut when the charge is rushing over the hill. At the end of the battle, we'll go home to a warm bed and decent food and people who love us, as many of those who really fought that battle never could. Why do we do what we do? To remember. To keep them alive in our hearts."

Dixie had always regarded reenactors as little boys indulging in pointless games. But what Kyle Sherman had described to her bore solemn witness to the lives and deaths of men caught up in the horrible war that had torn the nation asunder, a wrenching conflict that still had a direct bearing on the way many Southerners lived their lives today.

Kyle had captured her imagination, which was altogether too taxing at the moment. She was ready to rush out the door and back to the house. Her hand rested on the doorknob, then she turned back toward him. There was one thing she had to know.

"Your name," she blurted. "Kyle Sherman. It was General Sherman who earned the hatred of Southerners for all time. His foragers destroyed and pillaged, leaving people in their path, mostly wives and children, with no place to live and nothing to eat." She paused, trying to figure out if his blank stare meant that he was merely surprised or if it presaged something more severe—anger.

Kyle raised himself on one elbow as Dixie drew a deep breath. "Are you related to General Sherman in any way?" she asked all in a rush.

"Yes," he said gently. "He was my great-great-great-grand-father."

She nodded. He was more attractive than she had first discerned, and other than the sharp nose and large ears, he bore little resemblance to those pictures of General William Tecumseh Sherman in the history books. The tiny lamp by the bed illuminated his high cheekbones, dusted his lashes with gold.

She didn't say any more. Nothing else seemed relevant. She was deeply attracted to this man, to the sheer physicality of him and the soft reasoning way in which he spoke.

As she walked through the night back to the house, she pondered not only what Kyle had revealed about his heritage, which was startling enough to a girl who was Southern-born and –bred, but how he honored the soldiers who had fought and fallen in that long-ago war, and what it meant to him to do so.

Maybe the local United Daughters of the Confederacy chapter would have a hard time understanding how she could shelter a descendant of General William T. Sherman, yet for herself, it was time to let bygones be bygones. She had captured a Yankee, and she was determined to encourage him to stay around as long as he liked.

That decided, the only thing she had to figure out was whether to fix meat loaf or hamburgers for dinner.

Chapter Two

When Kyle Sherman woke up the next morning, he had the impression that he'd fallen down a rabbit hole. He recognized nothing about his charmingly rustic surroundings—not the teeny-tiny green-painted table decoupaged with pictures of kittens, not the tray sitting on the midget kitchen counter and certainly not the woman who was swinging down the path toward the little house.

She was gorgeous. Despite her well-rounded body parts, she was all glide and no jiggle. Her hair bounced around her shoulders, pale blond and gleaming as if spun from sunshine. Her face was a perfect oval, makeup tastefully applied, and she wore a pink dress, the hem of which was caught up at intervals with white ribbons, the better to show off shapely calves. Kyle used to be a boob man; nowadays he was strictly into legs, and this woman's were spectacular. He'd noticed them right off in the parking lot yesterday.

The memory reminded him how he happened to be here. The battle reenactment at Rivervale Bridge, his toothache, the subsequent root canal and the anesthetic knocking him for a loop. Then, and by far the most pleasant thing about that miserable day, the sweet angel of mercy who had gallantly came to his rescue and who right now was knocking on the quaint door to this Hobbity cottage where he lay naked beneath a quilt pieced of pastel calico.

"Come in," he said, wishing he'd had time to get dressed. His uniform was neatly spread over two of the teeny-tiny chairs, and he didn't recall putting it there. Maybe the woman had. He suddenly recalled that her name was Dixie, a perfect appellation for a perfect Southern belle.

"How are you feeling?" she asked, giving the impression that she really cared.

"Better."

"I'm going to church. When I get back, I'll take you to get your truck."

He shook his head in disbelief. "I can't believe what happened yesterday. I felt as if I was spinning off the end of the world when I was standing there in the parking lot. Thanks for helping me out."

"Like I said, I was glad to do it. I fixed scrambled eggs, grits and bacon for breakfast. I, um, suppose you're hungry?"

Because of his overwhelming urge to sleep, he'd barely sampled the meat loaf last night. "I could eat something," he allowed.

"I'll bring it out," she said, though her gaze fell doubtfully on the little table. He glanced out the window where a picnic table stood near the dock extending into the lake.

"How about if I eat outside? It's such a nice spring morning." He was in awe of the gorgeous reds of the azaleas, the dogwoods with their ethereal pink and white blossoms, the pale flowers of the ornamental Bradford pear trees trembling gently in the breeze.

As Dixie turned to go, he made a point of glancing at her left hand, though he didn't usually check. The third finger was ringless, which made him unexpectedly glad. He'd been in an off-and-on relationship with a woman named Andrea for a long time, but it was definitely off at present. Well, make that probably off, considering that she'd been leaving voice messages on his cell phone for the past three days. Not that he could have returned them even if he had the urge. His cell-phone service had been spotty ever since he'd crossed the state line into South Carolina.

He wasn't on the prowl for a new interest. On the other hand, he'd never met anyone as appealing as Dixie Lee Smith. When she disappeared up the path toward the house, he sprang out of bed. Last night he'd figured that when he woke up he'd feel as he did when he had a bad hangover. He expected to find a straggle-haired stranger staring back at him from the teeny-tiny mirror—hollow of cheek, dull of eye and seriously due for a shave. Aside from a bit of swelling along his jawline, he looked fine except for needing that shave.

Taking heart from his appearance, he hit the shower. Though water pressure was low, the hot water was the right temperature and the soap made satisfying suds. After the makeshift shower arrangements at the battle site, it felt great. He dried himself on fluffy white towels and pulled on the blue uniform pants. He didn't have a razor or any toiletries with him. He'd left them in his truck.

When he emerged from the bathroom, Dixie was standing at the door. "I set your plate on the picnic table," she said. "Would you like me to find you a T-shirt?"

"That would be great," he said. *Always the quick come-back.* Clever repartee was somehow out of his reach this morning, maybe on most mornings. He wished he had a line of patter guaranteed to get results with women, but he was a little rusty at present.

Dixie hurried away and came back with not only a shirt but a personal-care kit like the ones they provided on long airline flights. She noticed him studying the airline's logo and gave a little laugh.

"I had that left over from an overnight flight to Rome to visit my sister a couple of weeks ago. I didn't need the shaving kit," she said.

"Thanks," he said, meaning it. He hesitated for a moment, then plunged ahead. "You're not going to make me eat breakfast alone, are you?"

She seemed disconcerted. "I'm teaching Sunday school today. I can't be late," she said after a few seconds' delay.

"Sorry, I just thought—"

She didn't let him finish what he was going to say. "I could sit for a few minutes, I guess."

"I'd like that," he said. He smiled at her.

While he stayed behind in the playhouse to shave, Dixie perched primly on the end of one of the picnic benches. At his approach, she smiled tentatively. He sat down across from her and lifted the domed cover on his plate. "Just like from room service," he said with a grin.

"Some restaurant-supply items were in the house along with a whole lot of junk I haven't managed to throw away yet."

He mixed the grits with the bacon and a good-size lump of butter as he'd learned to do last week at the Reb reenactors' camp. Breakfast really tasted good in the fresh morning air. From here he could see more of the house, a large clapboard-and-shingle structure with big windows overlooking a wide lawn. Brick-bordered flower beds, sadly unkempt, were scattered here and there, and an artesian well bubbled into a rock-lined pool nearby. The land, which was dotted with pine and oak trees, sloped gently to the fringe of reeds bordering the wide lake.

"Can you tell me something about this area? I'm not familiar with it," he said.

"This is Pine Hollow Lake," Dixie told him. "You're in the sand hills of South Carolina. Many centuries ago, the Atlantic Ocean, which is now ninety miles to the east of us, rose right up to the ridge over there in the distance. When the nuclear plant was built here, Blue Creek was dammed to flood the hollow and that created the lake."

"There's a nuclear plant?"

She nodded and pointed out a distant white plume of smoke. "Way over there."

"What was in the hollow before they flooded it?"

"There're whole farms and houses down there under the water. It's kind of eerie, isn't it?"

He nodded and took another bite of grits. "What happened to the people?" he asked.

"The electric company paid them well for their land and relocated them. I can't say some of them were too happy about it, from what I've heard. Well, that's progress."

He considered what it must have been like for those folks to see their homes covered with water. He shook his head.

"Maybe progress isn't always good," he said.

She shrugged. "Without it, where would I be? Developers are building on the other side of the lake now, and I'm selling expensive homes to retirees who have recently discovered the area."

"That's what you do? Real estate?"

"I'm in sales, and I've discovered that I'm good at it. I'll take the exam for my broker's license as soon as possible, and then, who knows? I could own a business someday." She stood up and brushed a dried leaf off her dress. "Sorry, I've got to run. One thing about our pastor, he starts services on time."

"I understand," Kyle said, smiling up at her.

"See you later," she said, and he watched as she walked toward the garage. She had a bounce to her step and a sway to her hips that was most fetching.

Stop it, he told himself.

You could get to know more about her, said a wee small voice inside him, though he wasn't sure it would be wise to heed its counsel. On the other hand, what if it was time for a new life, new friends, a new perspective?

He finished his breakfast as he thoughtfully gazed out over the lake where cattails swayed gently in the breeze and a lone sailboat was tacking toward the far shore. In Ohio, spring had yet to be sprung, flowers had yet to bloom, and in some places, snow had yet to melt. Back home he had an apartment, a dracaena that needed watering and a landlady who insisted on mothering him. At the moment, the most important thing seemed to be the dracaena, which ought to tell him something about himself, his life and what he planned to do with it.

Back home was a situation that he was loath to face, but he wasn't ready to admit that yet even to himself. And so he daydreamed of buying a sailboat of his own and sailing it across Pine Hollow Lake without a care in the world and with a charming woman by his side.

She looked a lot like Dixie Lee Smith, but she could have been anybody. Anybody he didn't know.

WHEN DIXIE ARRIVED home from church, Kyle was weeding the flower beds.

She didn't notice him as she parked her Mustang in the detached garage, but as she walked toward the house, she stopped short at the sight of him wearing old khaki shorts that he'd found in a box labeled Church Charity Closet. The box had held other garments, none of which appeared as if they'd fit Dixie—a pair of boys' overalls, baby things, children's winter coats.

She stood there, hands on her hips and head cocked to one side. "Why, Kyle Sherman!" she exclaimed. "What on earth are you doing?"

"Work that needs to be done." He straightened and smiled at her, wiping the perspiration from his forehead.

"I certainly didn't expect you to hire on as my yard man," she said, but it was clear that she was pleased. She walked around the flower bed, studying it. "I plan to plant marigolds here, all colors," she said.

"That would be pretty," he said. "I figured that in this climate, you might be ready for planting."

"It'll be soon, but I'm not much of a gardener. My sister, Carrie, used to have the most beautiful plantings all around the home place. That's where she lived before she got married. She and her husband claim they're going to take up residence there, and I wouldn't be surprised if they do."

"That's the sister who lives in Rome?"

"She's only visiting there while her husband is on location. She's married to Luke Mason, the movie star. She met him when he was filming a movie here."

"I never knew anyone who married a movie star."

"It took everyone in our family by surprise."

Kyle knelt again, determined to finish this job before she made him leave. "I figure we can go get my truck after I'm through here. If you have time, I mean."

"I drove past the dentist's office on my way home from church. That sure is a different-looking truck you have, all that chrome and the boxy shape of it."

It wasn't the first time someone had been curious about the truck, a modified pickup. "I'm a farrier," he said.

"A what?"

"A horseshoer. I shoe horses. I carry equipment with me. Forge, anvil, grinders, horseshoes, things like that."

She appeared intrigued. "You're the first farrier I've ever met. Where do you work?"

"I have my own business and service stable horses, pets, a few mules here and there. I love what I do, and it fits in well with my hobby. I take care of the cavalry horses at the reenactments."

Dixie sat on a nearby tree stump. "Some of the things you said last night about reenactments—they touched me," she said. "Though I could do without your being related to General Sherman."

He glanced at her briefly, but kept weeding, tossing uprooted plants into an old bushel basket. "If it's any comfort, my great-grandfather was never formally acknowledged by the Sherman family. He was the illegitimate child of the general's unmarried son and took the Sherman name only after his father died."

"Oh. Is that a sore point?"

"Not to me, but you won't find our branch of the family on any genealogical charts."

She thought that over for a moment. "Um, where can I go to a reenactment?"

"In Camden there's an excellent one every fall. It's a Revolutionary War reenactment, so I don't participate, but you might enjoy it."

"The battle of Camden...didn't the Americans lose that one?"

He grinned. "I'm afraid so. You're up on your history lessons."

"I won a medal in eighth grade for the highest average in middle-school history courses. I was proud of it."

He stood up, surveyed the flower bed. He'd eliminated the weeds, but it still needed edging. "That's a whole lot better. I'd be glad to clear the weeds out of the other beds for you."

"Aren't we going to drive downtown to get your truck?"

"Well, sure." He leaned back, hands on his hips. "It's just that I don't really need to be anyplace special right away. I have another guy covering my business for me back in Ohio. In fact, I'd like to ride around the horse country near Camden, and if you're agreeable, maybe we could barter a few more days' lodging in your cottage for my work around the place."

"Yankee, you've got a deal."

He reached out his hand to shake hers then quickly withdrew it when he realized his was too dirty to touch anything but more weeds. "I guess I'd better take another shower," he said ruefully.

"Okay, I'm going to change clothes. I'll be going on to my grandmother's house for Sunday dinner." She hesitated, clearly unsure of her ground. "You could come with me if you like. It's nothing fancy, just a simple family meal, but you'll leave well fed."

"I'd like that," he said slowly. "I'd like it a lot."

Dixie aimed a smile at him, one that could knock a man over at twenty paces. Her skirt swung with a flirtatious flip as she started toward the house. "Be ready in half an hour, and I'll tell Memaw that there'll be one extra. We'll go get your truck first and drop it off here on our way to her house." She stopped and frowned, half turning around. "Another thing," she added. "While we're there, don't tell anyone your last name." She disappeared into the house, the door shutting firmly behind her.

What the heck does she mean, don't tell anyone your last name? Kyle wondered as he hefted the basket of weeds. Still puzzling over it, he went to check his cell phone. It still hadn't revived, but that was okay. Suddenly he didn't feel a need to be connected, and that was a freeing feeling. Whistling, he went inside to take a shower.

WHEN THEY WENT into town to retrieve Kyle's truck, Dixie put the top down on her convertible. Her hair ruffled in the wind, and they passed countless fields readied for spring planting. Dixie drove a little too fast for Kyle's taste, but she was a competent driver and he didn't object.

At the dentist's parking lot, she was curious to inspect his truck. "The cargo area's built on the chassis of a regular pickup," Kyle explained. "The sides and back open upward so I can get to my equipment."

He flipped up the rear hatch. "This makes shade where I stand to work if there isn't a tree or barn around." He also opened the sides, which lifted up like wings, so she could see the variety of horseshoes stacked on "trees" expressly made for that purpose. Racks and compartments held rasps and nails. He kept his equipment scrupulously neat and clean, and Dixie seemed impressed.

"Maybe I'll get to watch you shoe a horse someday," she said.

"Maybe you will," he told her, liking the idea.

They dropped his truck off next to the sasanqua hedge

beside her driveway, and Kyle slid back into the passenger side of the car. He wasn't quite sure what to expect at this gathering of the Smith clan, so Dixie explained about her family as they drove into the countryside.

"Our branch of Smiths have resided in the area since before the American Revolution," she told him. "Several of my ancestors fought in the War Between the States. Their names are engraved on the base of the statue of the Confederate soldier in Memorial Park downtown."

This was apparently the root of Dixie's reluctance to mention his last name to her family. Kyle didn't understand; generations had lived and died since the end of the Civil War. People should be over it. Still, twenty-nine years ago, because that's how old she said she was, someone had named this woman Dixie Lee to commemorate an ill-fated nation and its greatest general, Robert E. Lee.

Dixie kept talking. "Memaw Frances is my paternal grandmother. My daddy died some years ago of heart disease, and Mama was just plain prostrate with grief. Then, in a worst-case scenario, she suffered a fatal embolism shortly after we lost Daddy. I've no lack of relatives, so I have a large extended family. What my sister and I would have done without them, I can't imagine."

Kyle, whose father had retired to the Florida Keys where he earned a marginal living as a fishing guide and whose mother had run off with a magazine salesman not long after he was born, knew little about big families and said so.

"Why, I can't imagine not getting everyone together on Sundays like we do," she said with honest astonishment. "What on earth do you do instead?"

Kyle couldn't really answer that. Sunday was just like any

other day to him, only there were a lot more sports programs on TV. Sometimes Andrea stayed over, and they'd go out for breakfast, or he'd get together with his reenactor friends. He'd never considered that he was missing anything.

Along the way, Dixie pointed out the Smith family's old home place, a large Victorian house that belonged to her sister, Carrie, and her husband. About a quarter of a mile down the road, Frances Smith lived in a sprawling brick rancher at the end of a long driveway winding through a pecan grove.

He followed Dixie into the house. A picture of Ronald Reagan hung beside the door and a well-worn Bible lay on the hall table. Dixie's grandmother looked to be a spry eighty. The guests included Dixie's cousin Voncille, an ample-size redhead with a hearty laugh and a husband who barely spoke a word. The husband's name was Skeeter, and he and Voncille had four children, stair steps named Paul, Liddy, Amelia and Petey.

Claudia, Frances's sister, who was hard of hearing, had brought her unmarried son, Jackson, who immediately pulled Kyle aside and asked him if he liked to watch pornographic movies. Another male relative named Estill, hollow of chest and bald of head, lurked on the outskirts of the group, and Kyle had no idea what his relation was to anybody else, nor did anyone explain it.

The children were all extremely handsome and reasonably well behaved, excluding the younger girl, Amelia, who kept wailing that she wanted a Tootsie Roll, and *right now, please.* No one paid any attention to her. Kyle considered suggesting that he run to the nearest convenience store and buy her the Tootsie Roll just to shut her up, then decided that if her parents didn't care about her whining, he should try to get used to it.

After he brushed off the question from Jackson about the porn movies, Kyle tried to stick close to Dixie, which meant that he was recruited to snap the ends off green beans while she fried the chicken. Memaw Frances busied herself mashing potatoes by hand, and once she'd eliminated all the lumps to her satisfaction, she dug around in the pantry for pickled okra that she never found.

"Memaw didn't make pickled okra last year," Voncille whispered to Dixie and Kyle on her way to the refrigerator to pour juice for Petey. "She keeps forgetting is all."

Frances's big lace-covered walnut table provided plenty of room for everyone, and it was set with fine china and crystal. Dixie seemed to take everything in stride, including being seated next to the profoundly deaf Claudia, who had to be told everything twice, even if it was only to please pass the salt. Kyle was seated on Frances's right, which meant that he had to endure a spate of tough questions while steering her away from queries about his name. Not only that, Dixie had also suggested quite strongly that he not mention the reenactment at Rivervale Bridge or the fact that he'd worn a blue Yankee uniform.

Kyle didn't like to meet Dixie's family or anyone else and not be able to tell them who he was, but he honored her request. That wasn't difficult to do when he recalled that while riding in the car with her to get his truck a while ago, her hand had so softly brushed his arm as she reached to slide the key into the ignition. His skin had crinkled into goose bumps at her touch and he wondered what would happen if their skin made contact again.

"YOU'RE FROM WHERE, CAL?" Claudia shouted across the table, knotting her face into a frown that rolled lines of pink powder from wrinkle to wrinkle.

"OHIO," he shouted back, unsure whether to correct Claudia's pronunciation of his name.

"And then I told her, 'Hon, I'm not going to any shower for the daughter of a woman who cut me dead when Skeeter and I had to get married,'" Voncille was telling Dixie.

"Can I have more chicken?" asked Paul, and Voncille forked a drumstick onto his plate without losing a beat in her monologue.

"You ever heard of Linda Lovelace?" Jackson asked Estill, who remained bowed over his plate and kept spooning mashed potatoes into his mouth, which appeared deficient in teeth.

"And your mother's maiden name was *what?*" Frances asked Kyle with interest.

"Oh, you wouldn't know his people, Memaw," Dixie volunteered hastily. "By the way, this is the best cranberry relish you've ever made."

"Let me tell you how I make it so you can do it yourself. I take my food grinder—that's the old crank one that Mama had when she first married—and I wash the cranberries real good, getting all the dirt and leaves off. Then I—"

"I intended to send a present, but right off I changed my mind, money being tight and Skeeter being jobless again," Voncille said. "Maybe I'll just mail a card after the baby's born, whether Jenny gets married or not."

"Listen, dumbhead, stop kicking me under the table," Liddy told her brother, who reached for the creamed corn and managed to spill it down the front of his shirt, whereupon Skeeter, his father, sent him to the bathroom to clean it off.

"You grind up the nuts medium-coarse, and pecans are best," Frances went on. "Lord knows I've got enough pecans from my trees, that is, if the squirrels don't get them all."

"Did you say you were from Iowa?" Voncille asked Kyle politely.

"Get all the little pieces of shell off the nuts before you grind them. You could break a tooth otherwise."

Kyle kept munching on his third piece of fried chicken. He'd heard that Southerners really had a way with fried chicken, but he wouldn't have believed it could be so light and crispy.

"They've got this back room at the video store, it's for adults only," Jackson was telling Skeeter enthusiastically.

Voncille shot a warning glance in his direction and addressed him in an undertone that everyone heard anyway. "Jackson, *there are children present.* Please talk about something else."

"I didn't get any mashed potatoes, Mom. Can you put gravy on? Who's Linda Lovelace?" Paul asked.

"Kyle shoes horses. It's what he does for a living," Dixie explained to someone, Kyle wasn't sure who.

"HE *SHOOTS* HORSES? WHAT KIND OF JOB IS THAT?" Claudia asked, and Kyle almost choked on a mouthful of iced tea.

"Kyle *shoes* horses, Aunt Claudia," Liddy said in her loudest voice.

Frances blinked off into the distance for a moment. "I had a horse when I was a child. His name was Booster. Now, how come I can remember that horse's name when I can't even recall where I put the pickled okra?"

"I carry everything I need for shoeing a horse around in my truck," Kyle told Liddy who stared at him entranced.

"The horse, too?"

"No, not the horse, the horseshoes and the equipment I use to attach the shoes to their hooves."

"Daddy, *when* can I have a Tootsie Roll?" Amelia chimed in.

"Hush up, Amelia."

"You use big long nails, right?"

"Does it hurt the horse?" Paul asked.

"And then I fold in the cranberries, just so."

"Uncle Estill, would you like to go to the video store with me sometime? Next week, maybe?" Jackson asked despite a glare from Voncille. Still gumming mashed potatoes, Estill gave no sign that he'd heard.

"I KNEW SOME KALBS OVER NEAR LAURENS," Claudia shouted. "A BIG FAMILY. THEY OWNED A CAR DEALERSHIP."

"No relation," Kyle said.

"And then all you have to do is put it in the refrigerator and eat it," Frances said, though Kyle was sure that by this time, no one was listening.

It went on like this until all the fried chicken and mashed potatoes were gone, which was when Voncille pushed back her chair. "Well, I guess we're all finished eating. Is anyone ready for fudge cake? I brought one along."

Estill raised his head and spoke for the first time. "I'd like some cake, Vonnie, but first I'll have some of that pickled okra. Can you mash it up real good?"

"I told you, Estill, I couldn't *find* the pickled okra," Frances said with great patience.

"Come on out to the kitchen, Memaw, I'll help you search for it," Liddy said comfortably as she slid off her chair. She took Frances's hand and the two of them disappeared.

Kyle caught Dixie's eye and was surprised to recognize an amused glint there. He smiled back, and she shrugged lightly as if to say she couldn't help it, this was her family and she loved them.

Though he was lacking in family himself, her attitude struck Kyle as really important. Some people would be embarrassed by the carryings on and eccentricities of the people involved. However, Dixie had made it plain that she was not. Maybe more than anything else, Kyle liked this about her.

WHEN THE TWO OF THEM arrived back at Dixie's place after dinner, Kyle wished she wouldn't go inside right away. He had no desire to spend the rest of the evening alone contemplating the sexual sparks that seemed to fly between them.

"I had a good time," he said. "Thanks for inviting me."

"Oh, we're a fun bunch, all right," Dixie said with an amused laugh. "Life wouldn't be the same without my family especially now that my sister's moved away." She seemed pensive as she pulled a jacket closer around her in order to fend off the cool night wind that soughed through the pine trees.

Impulse took over, making him bolder. "Let's walk out on the dock and you can tell me how your sister happened to marry Luke Mason," he said. He liked Luke Mason's movies, which generally consisted of snappy dialogue, an attractive cast and a couple of improbable car chases. Plus, a discussion down on the dock might lead to something far more interesting.

He was delighted when Dixie said, "If you like," though he cautioned himself against getting his hopes up. They walked together across the grass, past the flower bed he'd cleared earlier and onto the dock. Several loose boards could use nailing down, he noticed in the light of the full moon, and certainly one or two needed to be replaced.

When they reached the dock's end, they leaned companionably side by side on the railing where the moon path on the water rippled toward the opposite shore. The air was fragrant with the scent of green growing things and another indefinable fragrance that Kyle suspected was Dixie's shampoo.

"Would you really like to hear about my sister and Luke Mason?" she asked.

"Of course," he replied easily. Suddenly it seemed as if everything about her interested him.

With a wistful half smile she said, "Carrie and Luke Mason are a love story that was meant to be. She didn't figure it out right away, it took her a while. Oh, when she realized—well, she blossomed. Bloomed."

Kyle was slightly uncomfortable with this topic because love had certainly never done that for him, but he'd rather not destroy Dixie's romantic notions. He wasn't required to comment, however, because she went on talking.

"Luke Mason was here to film a movie, *Dangerous*. It'll be released next summer. It's about our local stock-car-racing hero, Yancey Goforth, and how he came out of nowhere to become one of the greatest race-car drivers of all time."

"I've read something about the movie. Doesn't it have a more serious plot than his earlier films?"

"Carrie says he may be nominated for an Academy Award, it's that good."

"He's an underrated actor, in my opinion."

"They filmed part of the movie in Smitty's, my sister's garage, because it offered the ambience of the era when Yancey was getting started in stock-car racing. In fact, Yancey and my grandfather were friends. A couple of weeks before Carrie signed a contract with the movie company, I tried to talk her into converting the garage into a real estate office so we could go into business together, but she refused. Our dad left her the garage and the home place and me enough money to take a real estate course and put a down payment on my house."

"How can your sister keep her business if she's married to a movie star?"

"She sold Smitty's to her mechanic. She retired so she could travel with Luke, and she wants to bear his children." This was said dramatically, though Dixie was smiling. "Who wouldn't?" she added wryly.

"You've got a point there," he agreed.

"How about you, Kyle? Ever been married? Have any children?"

He shook his head. "No, unfortunately." The last angry quarrel with Andrea two weeks ago still rankled; she'd informed him that even if they got married, which according to her was most unlikely, she didn't want kids.

Dixie gazed out over the water, and he began to suspect that she didn't discuss personal things with strangers. Why she'd chosen to so honor him, he couldn't imagine, but something inside him opened to her.

"I've never been married, either," she said. "I wish—but you don't need to hear about that."

In his time, Kyle had lent an ear to women who bemoaned the fact that they weren't getting any younger but hadn't found the right partner yet and to several others who belatedly wished they'd borne children in marriages that had ended in divorce. Usually he tried to steer them away from the topic. However, with Dixie, he was eager to learn more.

"Try me," he said, gazing down at her.

"I could have married young, to my high-school boyfriend. I sent Milo away, and he never came back." She seemed pensive but stoic in the manner of someone who had given a great deal of consideration to whether she'd done the right thing.

"That's too bad," he said automatically, but was it?

"A marriage between us would have been a disaster," she said.

"That depends on if you'd been able to grow together," Kyle suggested mildly.

Dixie slanted a glance up at him. "Do you consider that important? Learning and growing with a life partner, I mean?"

"Of course," he answered, unable and unwilling to stop himself. "Shared experiences are the glue that holds two people together."

Dixie leaned closer, which might have been by accident or design, he couldn't tell which. Or maybe the rough railing was sticking a splinter into her arm, a distinct possibility if a person wasn't careful.

She easily resumed the thread of conversation. "Take my cousin Voncille and her husband, Skeeter, for instance. They got married when she was seventeen, and she dropped out of school to work until their baby was born. She'll tell you herself that when they started out, she had a lot to learn about marriage and children. Even though they don't have much money, there's a lot of love in that family. Together Voncille and Skeeter are both better people than they would have been apart."

Kyle didn't often get the chance to state his own opinions about relationships and how they worked. He usually left that to someone else. But if he had been in the habit of saying what he wanted or needed from a woman, he would have said that two people together should be halves of one whole. That each of them should help the other become the best person he or she could be. Dixie's understanding of this principle not only surprised him, it validated his thinking. He was silent for so long that Dixie studied him out of the corner of her eye for a long moment before speaking.

"I haven't said anything to offend you, have I?" she ventured.

He cleared his throat. "No."

"For a while there, I wondered."

"I, uh, well. Of course I'm not offended," he said. *Where have you been all my life?* he was thinking.

He liked her way too much, and maybe she was assuming things that she shouldn't. He wasn't ready to enmesh himself in another situation where there was no getting out, yet he was thirty-two years old and ready to settle down.

Dixie was gazing up at him, the moon reflected in her blue, blue eyes, her eyelashes casting feathery shadows across her cheeks. He longed to run his hands under her sweet-smelling hair, press his body close to hers and whisper her name softly in her ear. *Don't do this,* he told himself. *Stop it. Don't.* Not that any relevant part of him was listening.

Dixie saw his intent, and she did not back away. Even though he'd known her only a bit longer than twenty-four hours, even though when they'd met, he'd been wearing a Yankee uniform, even though she knew nothing about him other than what he'd seen fit to relate.

"Oh, Kyle," she said, exhaling his name on a long breath. Before she could tell him to stop, he did what was possibly the stupidest thing in his life, considering that he quite possibly still had a girlfriend back in Ohio. He swept Dixie Lee Smith into his arms and kissed her.

Chapter Three

Dixie's desk was situated at the very front of the Yewville Real Estate Company's office where she could watch people walking past and greet them when they came in. That's because she had started out as an administrative assistant to Jim Terwilliger, the broker in charge, and his wife, Mayzelle, who liked to help out around the office too often to suit everyone else. Mayzelle *meant* well and had a kind heart, everyone agreed. They just could do with a good bit less of her advice and company.

Right now Mayzelle was on the phone with Glenda at the Curly Q Beauty Salon discussing what to do about her botched hair color, which was supposed to be Desert Dream, but had turned out more like Copper Kettle. She was trying to talk Glenda into working her in immediately.

"Maybe Rose Inglett would switch with me? She's done it before when it suits her," Mayzelle said. "I mean, most people would give anything for my Friday slot?"

Dixie, who was inserting new pages in her listing book, tried to concentrate on her task. It wasn't easy, considering Mayzelle's distracting conversation and the fact that last night Dixie had been kissed by possibly the best kisser she'd ever encountered. Who knew that Yankees could kiss like that? It pained her to learn what she'd been missing all these years.

Dixie had done her share of making out in her time, and she'd even had a serious boyfriend or two or three. Well, okay, make that four. First Milo Dingle, the boy she'd been engaged to be engaged to in high school. Then Rob Portner, the guy who delivered firewood to everyone in town. And after that, Thad Ganey, who'd gone and enlisted in the navy. Last, and definitely least, Sam Hodges, who'd run off with Tattin Kelly when they were all staying in a rented condo at the beach last Fourth of July. The thing with Sam still rankled, since he'd neglected to pay his share of the condo rental. Plus, Dixie had loaned Tattin her best beach cover-up for the weekend and never got it back. If she'd known those two had the hots for each other, she'd have made sure Tattin borrowed the cover-up with the peach-juice stain down the front.

"Dixie Lee," Mayzelle said, interrupting her reverie. "I'm going to run over to Glenda's for a bit? I should only be an hour or so. You don't mind answering the phones, do you?"

"No, Mayzelle, you go right ahead." Anything to get Mayzelle out of the office for a while; she tended to drive everyone crazy with her high voice and the annoying habit of ending almost every sentence with a question mark.

Mayzelle woke Fluffy, her elderly poodle, who slept under her desk, and with the unresisting dog tucked firmly under her arm, she exited the office, leaving Dixie alone.

Dixie intended to write letters to a couple of friends who had shipped out with the Guard unit. As it turned out, all she did was replay last night's kiss in her mind. She took out a pen and paper. She even addressed the envelopes. Before she had a chance to get started on the letters, the phone rang.

"Dixie," said her friend Joyanne calling from California where she'd lived ever since getting her big break in the Luke Mason movie and embarking on a new career as an actress. "I only have a minute before I leave for an audition, but I heard Milo Dingle is back in town. Have you seen him yet?"

"No, and I don't expect I will," Dixie said, pulling up her e-mail screen on the computer. Sure enough, there were two messages with Milo's name in the subject line, so the Yewville grapevine was in gear.

"Don't be so sure. Milo told my cousin Norm's wife, Betty, that he's going to renew his acquaintance with you. He asked her to get your phone number."

"Milo knows where to find me, not that I care," Dixie said. "Right about the tenth pew, lefthand side, in church every Sunday. In fact, that's exactly where he left me twelve years ago."

"Milo didn't leave you," Joyanne said. "I distinctly recall that he asked you to marry him shortly after the collection plate passed by, and you said no. Milo was ambivalent about joining his father on the family peach farm so he moved to Kingstree to help his uncle grow daylilies for Wal-Mart is all. Since you declined to go with him, that does not qualify as leaving you."

"I've never regretted my decision."

"It would have been a beautiful wedding," Joyanne said wistfully. "All those daylilies."

"I was ready to go out with other guys," she told Joyanne, not that this was real news.

"Speaking of guys, have you heard from Sam?"

"Sam the Mooch and Tattin are planning their wedding. They're having two singers, eight candelabra and a string quartet at the First Baptist Church in Florence."

"Has Sam paid you his share of the condo rent yet?"

"He never will, the cheapskate. He liked to let me cover the tab at the Eat Right Café, and I filled his SUV with gas more than once. I wonder why I put up with it for so long."

"It was only a couple of months, Dixie."

"A couple of months too long. It's some consolation that Tattin will have to deal with him for the rest of her life." She paused. "How are things going with you?"

"I'm up for a part in a family drama for the Lifetime channel," Joyanne said. "It's a cross between *Little House on the Prairie* and *Little Women*."

"All that 'Little,'" Dixie said. "I hope it's not only a little money."

"If I get the gig, I'll be able to buy my own place."

"Good for you, Joyanne," Dixie said warmly, finding *gig* an odd new word in her friend's vocabulary.

"What's up with you? Anything important? How did your tooth whitening go?"

"Good. I got two fillings, as well." She didn't mention Kyle Sherman.

"Is that the end of your self-improvement program?"

"I'm not sure. Now that I've got a new wardrobe for my job, my hair professionally highlighted and my eyeliner tattooed on, I may be through." Dixie didn't believe she was vain, exactly, but she was twenty-nine years old and competition for husbands was stiff these days. She'd merely done what she could to maximize her chances in a town where for every hundred females over the age of eighteen, there were only seventy-one males, many of them away in the military or way over the age of sixty.

Joyanne chuckled. "You couldn't be anything but gorgeous, trust me. Look, I've got to run. Talk to you soon, Dixie. Call me if you hear from Milo."

"Uh-huh."

They hung up, and Dixie opened her e-mails. One was from Voncille, who had typed a few lines about Skeeter's running into Milo at the Eat Right that morning. Another was from Milo's sister, Priss, who invited Dixie to stop by her house for coffee next Saturday. Dixie was quite sure this was no mere coincidence since she hadn't seen or talked with Priss for ages.

So back to last night. She and Kyle had kissed with the moonlight beaming down so bright it hurt her eyes, which was why she'd closed them as his lips met hers. He had the softest lips. They were firm, too, and he used them to elicit the most exciting sensations. She'd swooned into the kiss, every part of her body primed for more as he used his mouth to tell her how much he wanted her without saying a word. It was a long kiss, that first one, followed by several more, or perhaps it was one kiss broken into several parts because once they'd started neither of them tried to stop. She'd been tipsy only a couple of times in her life, and this reminded her of that loose, dizzy, confused feeling. It was even better though, because instead of falling asleep as she always did after too much to drink, this time, she was fully alert, aroused and ready.

It probably wasn't the wisest thing in the world to be deeply kissing a man she'd just met. She'd told herself to put a stop to it right then and there. Only, what harm was there in indulging herself for once in her life, as she did by eating a chocolate bar now and then? Kyle T. Sherman would soon be on his way back to Ohio, and she'd never see him again. Never kiss him again.

Last night she'd instinctively looped her hands around Kyle's neck, pulling him closer until their bodies came into contact. Electrified, she made no objection when he tangled his fingers in her hair, when he cupped her face, his big hands rough against her cheeks. She couldn't remember ever kissing anyone with so much feeling and longing. Certainly it had never been that way with Milo or Sam or any of the others. She'd let them take the lead, but with Kyle, she'd be satisfied with nothing less than the whole sexual experience. Longed to lie naked with him in the shadows of the oaks near the edge of the lake. Anticipated guiding him into her and being possessed by him, his flesh hammering her into total surrender. It was bewildering to feel such a strong yearning, one that seemed likely to deprive her of all control.

So if they'd kept on kissing, where might it have ended? However, as things were heating up to the next level, they heard a raucous cry, then a large bird swept out of nowhere, its wings nearly brushing their cheeks as it passed. They sprang apart, both startled.

"I wasn't expecting that," Kyle said ruefully. His hand still rested on her shoulder, but the mood was broken and they had awkwardly moved apart.

Due to the untimely interruption, good sense returned, and she'd told Kyle that she'd better get a decent night's sleep because she had clients to meet the next morning. When they reached the end of the dock, he shook her hand, which was really laughable considering their passionate kissing only a few moments past. He'd told her again how much he'd enjoyed spending the afternoon with her family. Then, her lips still tingling from his kisses, she'd fled into the house, where she leaned against the back door and fanned herself into a semblance of normality with a church program.

She hadn't seen Kyle this morning when she'd headed to work. What he chose to do with his day was no business of hers. Except now that she'd developed a craving for his kisses and a hankering to learn not only how far she'd go but how far he would, she was determined that they'd both have a chance to find out.

While she was still lost in remembrance of last night, Dixie's boss returned to the office and inquired how her two showings that morning had gone.

While she was filling him in, Mayzelle walked in with her poodle and started heating up a Lean Cuisine in the microwave in the break room. Two other agents arrived, excitedly discussing the current ad for the old textile mill in the *Wall Street Journal,* and Dixie fielded a call from a man who had discovered one of her listings on the Internet and asked if the house had a bonus room where he and his wife could raise Maine coon cats. Never a dull moment, Dixie told herself as she headed out to show one of the new houses up on the lake to the man with the cats.

Just the same she sure wished she knew what Kyle Sherman was up to.

AFTER HE CLEANED OUT the remaining three flower beds and fired up the Weedwacker to trim the overgrown grass at the edges of the driveway, Kyle treated himself to a long cool drink of water from the artesian well on Dixie's property. The water bubbled up out of a pipe sunk into the earth and into a

pool made by piling rocks in a circle. The water was clean
and cold and pure, though some of the rocks had crumbled
or were missing. They needed to be replaced and arranged in
a downhill pattern so the pool could become a pretty little waterfall. He'd like to do that for Dixie if he stuck around long
enough.

He tried to call his friend Elliott, with whom he'd tented
at the reenactment. He wanted to let Elliott know that he was
okay, but his cell phone was still not working. In the meantime, he noticed that the sky was a bright china blue with no
clouds in sight. The lake crested in tiny waves driven by the
warm breeze, and after cooling off, Kyle had an itch to get
out and about, to explore this place where he had landed
through no planning of his own.

He intended his driving tour to encompass downtown
Yewville and leave it at that. Smitty's Garage and Gas Station
seemed to be doing a good business with cars lined up at the
pumps. And at the town's only traffic light, drivers saluted
each other by raising a forefinger and nodding solemnly. The
one depressing sight was the old Yewville Mill building,
closed and shuttered. A For Sale sign hung on the chain-link
fence that surrounded it and weeds grew up through cracks
in the sidewalk. Someone had scrawled Moved To Mexico
on the brick wall in front of the administration building.

His turn about Yewville took seven minutes total, beginning to end, after which he wasn't of a mood to go back to
his Hobbit cottage. Besides, he was hungry, so he stopped at
the Eat Right Café.

It was a small storefront restaurant with red-and-white
checked vinyl cloths tacked to the tables in the booths. The
servers, all women, wore pink uniforms with bright handker-

chiefs blossoming from their chest pockets, reminding Kyle of pictures he'd seen of 1940s diners. He sat down at the long black counter and checked out the menu stuck between the sugar shaker and napkin holder.

His waitress, who wore a name tag announcing herself as Kathy Lou, favored him with a great big smile as she came to take his order. "You must be the Yankee who's staying in that old playhouse out there at Dixie Smith's new place on the lake," she said.

"How'd you know that?" he asked mildly, noting that chicken bog was today's blue-plate special and wondering what in the world chicken bog could be.

"Word gets around."

"Amazing. What's chicken bog?"

"Local specialty," Kathy Lou said. "Some people calls it chicken and rice, more soupy than the usual. I don't recollect where the bog came from, 'less it's because somebody was trying to impress people that we have a lot of swamp around here, though I'm not sure why anyone would want to do *that*, considering that all the swamp ever produced was Lizard Man, and it was a long time ago anybody saw him."

"All right, I'll order the chicken bog, only if you tell me about Lizard Man," Kyle told her, and she laughed.

"Around here we figure the less said about it, the better," she told him as she dished up a plate of chicken and rice. "It involved a teenager riding home through Scape Ore Swamp with a mess of fried chicken in a take-home bucket on the seat beside him. This thing rushed out of the swamp while the kid was changing a tire, and he said it looked like a cross between a lizard and a man. It tried to steal his chicken dinner. They never found the creature, if that's what you're wondering."

She started a fresh pot of coffee as the lunch crowd began to converge on the only eatery in town.

Kyle thanked Kathy Lou for the chicken bog recommendation and the Lizard Man story before leaving. As he walked out the door, several other servers clustered around Kathy Lou to "ooh" and "aah" over his magnanimous tip. He was secretly amused and made up his mind to leave an even larger one next time he stopped in.

He rode back down Palmetto Street, spotting Dixie framed in the big window strung across the front of the Yewville Real Estate Company office. She was talking on the phone in an animated fashion, and she was beautiful.

He wasn't sure what to make of her. Usually he was a stickler for the accepted pacing of a relationship. In other words, first he'd call the woman in whom he'd developed an interest. Then he'd schmooze her, ask her out, and if his luck held, bed her by the third date. Yet with Dixie, he wanted to move faster than that. Dixie seemed to return his interest four times over, if he was any judge of women.

As he pondered this, he found himself on the highway driving toward the town of Camden. He smiled at Yewville's famous peachoid water tower as he passed it his way out of town. Dolly's, a truck stop out on the bypass, was doing a brisk business. A short distance down the road, a decrepit motel advertised ROOMS $6 AN HOUR WEEKLY $85 CLEAN SHEETS. After that, the countryside was mostly flat and canopied with trees rising lush and green on both sides of the narrow highway.

Before long, he found himself singing along with the radio station billing itself as "WYEW, Yew-and-Me Country." When he realized what he was doing, he quit singing, surprised at himself. It had been a long time since he'd spontaneously sung out loud, but it was a release of something pent up inside him for far too long.

Kyle's first impression upon entering Camden, South Carolina, was that it offered more small-town sameness of the sort he'd found in Yewville. As a history buff, however, he was aware of Camden's historical significance in two wars, the American Revolution and the Civil War, so he set out to discover some of its rich history.

He found the town full of picturesque houses. One of them, the Joshua Reynolds House, was one of the oldest buildings in town. Kyle was interested to learn that it was once owned by Dr. George R.C. Todd, a Confederate surgeon who was also the brother of Mary Todd Lincoln, wife of Abraham Lincoln, a situation that must have provoked more than a few interesting discussions around the dinner table at the White House.

After his historical tour, it was sheer luck that led him to the polo field. A man who introduced himself as Jarvis Wilfield interrupted his chore of loading horses into a trailer to walk over and talk. He was most interested in what Kyle did for a living.

"A horseshoer, huh?" Wilfield said, squinting up at Kyle, who towered over him by at least a foot. Wilfield was a stumpy little man with a contagious grin. "We could use a good farrier around here. See, a lot of Northerners come to Camden during the winter because the weather is warmer than New York, New Jersey and some of them other places. They bring their horses, they play polo, they practice jumping or whatever. Some of them, they think more of their horses than of people."

Kyle laughed at this, but he admired horses, too, and understood why people connected with them in a special way. "Don't you have a local horseshoer?" Kyle asked, taking in the wide flat field and miscellaneous outbuildings.

"Yeah, but Mac McGehee is getting old. Wants to retire, but we won't let him." Wilfield smiled. "If you was around, Mac might get to buy that fishing boat and hang out at Santee pulling in bass and crappie hand over fist."

"I'd like to talk to him sometime." Kyle knew there was always a lot to learn from the old-timers in the business.

Wilfield shot him a keen-eyed look. "You interested in working as his assistant?"

Kyle shook his head. "I'm a full-time journeyman farrier. I have a business in Ohio."

"Ever consider moving south?"

"Not really." *It's beginning to seem like a great idea, considering the charms of Dixie Lee Smith.*

"There's work here if you're interested."

"I appreciate your telling me that," Kyle said. He liked the guy, who reminded him of his mentor when he'd first started shoeing horses.

"Maybe you'd better give me your phone number. Mac might like to talk with you."

Kyle's cell phone still refused to work, so he scribbled the number of Dixie's landline on one of his regular business cards. That morning, she'd left a note instructing him that the back door of the house was always open and to use her phone whenever he liked.

Wilfield wrote his name and address on a page ripped from his notepad and handed it over. "You can always find me at the stable."

"Thanks. I appreciate this," Kyle said.

Wilfield waved goodbye and then drove off, stirring a flurry of yellow dust in his wake.

Afterward, Kyle ambled around the polo field thinking about the man's suggestion that he take over Mac McGehee's business. The trouble was, Camden, South Carolina, was a far cry from Ohio. The climate here was different, the food was different, the people didn't talk the way he did and sometimes he couldn't understand their accent. He'd be an outsider here. He had a good business back in Ohio. So why would he decide to start anew in a place that was so different from that to which he was accustomed? Adventure? Excitement? Challenge? He couldn't, no matter how hard he tried, answer the question honestly.

A possible move wasn't what was on his mind during the ride back to Yewville. He was bemused by how eager he was to see Dixie. When he arrived back at the house on the lake, he spotted her through her kitchen window as soon as he pulled to a stop in the driveway. She was wearing an apron, the picture of domesticity. Her cheeks were rosy from the heat of the stove, and a stray curl bobbed over her forehead. In fact, she made such an appealing picture that he hesitated for a moment on the back steps before knocking on the door.

She threw the door open, welcoming him with a big smile.

"My goodness, I'm glad you're back," she said. "When you weren't here, I thought maybe you'd left town for good." If he wasn't mistaken, that was an expression of relief on her face.

"No," he said, gazing down at her and thinking that leaving Yewville would have been even more stupid than kissing her last night, which had turned out to be one of the best things he'd done since he arrived. He was unaccustomed to making a person's eyes light up when he walked in a room, and he found that he liked it a lot.

"Then I realized you make friends easily and had probably found something fun to do. So did you go in search of Lizard Man?"

"What gave you that idea?"

"Kathy Lou at the Eat Right said she filled you in about our local legend. A couple of other people who were there at the time corroborated that you were mighty interested."

Kyle shook his head, amazed at how fast a minor conversation in his life had been overreported.

Dixie grinned. "Just in case you have any hope of resurrecting Lizard Man, I might as well tell you that a lot of people doubt that he ever existed, me included."

"Nope, I wasn't chasing local legends. Instead I drove over to Camden for the day."

"Tell me about it while we eat dinner," she said as if it was a given that he'd been invited. Thus Kyle found himself sitting at the kitchen table, pouring out the details of his day.

"So I was thinking," he said as he wound up his summary, "what are houses going for in the area? I mean, what would it actually cost to live around here?" It was the last thing he'd anticipated asking, yet it seemed perfectly natural.

Dixie seemed surprised at the question, though she couldn't be as surprised as he was himself. "How many bedrooms would you need?" she asked. "How many baths?"

"At least three bedrooms and two baths, I suppose." He envisioned using one bedroom for himself, another for a den, and setting up the third one for an exercise room.

Dixie named a price that surprised him; property values

here were lower than in Ledbetter, and that meant lower taxes, too. "If you like," Dixie continued, "I can show you some homes."

"Great!" He beamed at her over the dinner table.

"It's the least I can do considering the work you did in the yard this morning. I was hoping I'd get a chance to tackle it, but I haven't had much time lately what with just moving in." She lifted her shoulders and let them fall expressively before getting up and starting to clear the table.

So far Dixie hadn't indicated by actions or manner that she recalled what had happened between them last night. Kyle had the urge to walk up behind her and wrap his arms around her, letting his hands mold the soft curves of her breasts.

No. That wouldn't do. Coming on strong would turn her against him completely.

"I was thinking," he said slowly, "that some ice cream would taste good right now. A big dish of it, your favorite flavor."

She blinked like a doe caught in the headlights, or was something else going on here? A wish that they skip the ice cream and find another way to amuse themselves? Of course, this might be hoping for too much. Perhaps he wasn't reading the situation correctly, though something had changed between them. Dixie's pupils had gone dark, her lips had taken on a sultry droop instead of curving upward in her usual smile, and she'd dropped the dish towel.

He'd learned from all those battle reenactments that sometimes you had to sound a retreat to convince the opposing side to move in your direction. "Hey," he said softly, "if I'm in the way, tell me. I'd rather not overstep any boundaries."

"Ice cream sounds great," she said.

"What kind?"

"Pistachio. Or cherry vanilla. I really don't care."

"I'll surprise you," he said cheerfully on his way out the door.

YOU ALREADY HAVE, Dixie thought to the accompaniment of his engine starting and his subsequent departure. *Surprised me by broadening my horizons, making me think about things I never considered, such as why reenactors do what they do, and showing me consideration and kindness.*

That was the clincher. In the many snippets of advice Memaw Frances had sent Dixie's way, her admonition to find a man who was, above all, kind and considerate stuck in her mind. When Dixie was younger, she'd had in mind to find a handsome guy whose genes could be transmitted to their beautiful children. She'd wanted someone who could dance, who liked to laugh and took his financial obligations seriously. All those things were still important, no doubt about that. Still, if a man wasn't kind and considerate, day-to-day life could get pretty grim. If he didn't challenge her to think, their marriage would be boring. If he didn't have a passion for his work or his hobbies, chances were that he wouldn't be able to muster passion for much else, either. Including, possibly, the woman in his life.

So. She'd better check her makeup, decide if she needed more lipstick. Break out the mouthwash. Find that bottle of perfume she'd buried in a box of bathroom supplies.

Thank goodness she didn't have to worry about eyeliner. Unlike many other things in life, her tattooed eyeliner was permanent. Her teeth were a newly bright and sparkly white. And her hair had never looked better.

Ignore all that, Kyle Sherman, and you're crazy.

When you'd maximized your chances the way she'd done,

you had a right to expect results. And she was sure she'd see some—plus a lot of other interesting things—tonight.

THE BI-LO SUPERMARKET was only a short drive away. Kyle rushed through the store, scooped ice cream out of the freezer and seethed when the customer ahead of him at the checkout insisted on laboriously counting out change.

When he arrived back at Dixie's house, she looked as if she'd run a brush through her hair, maybe even refreshed her lipstick. She'd set out two bowls, and he opened the carton of cherry-vanilla ice cream. As he scooped it into the bowls. headlights swung across the trees outside. "Are you expecting anyone?" he asked, figuring the visitor was one of Dixie's numerous relatives.

"No," Dixie said blankly. She moved to the door for a better view. "Oh, drat. I don't believe it. Of all the bad timing."

Playing it casually, Kyle licked a runnel of ice cream from his finger and went to peer at the figure approaching the back steps. "Who is it, anyway?"

She darted him a wary look. "My former boyfriend," she said. "Milo."

THEIR VISITOR REMINDED Kyle of something, though at first he didn't know what it was. Then it occurred to him that Milo resembled his childhood teddy bear after the stuffing had started to get lumpy and fall out. The man had round cheeks, chubby hands and an abundance of curly brown hair, not to mention the beginning of a paunch under his neatly pressed plaid shirt.

Kyle tried to recall what Dixie had told him about the relationship. He didn't recall if she'd said why a marriage between them would have been a mistake, yet she'd seemed firm enough in her belief. So what was the guy doing here?

As Kyle busied himself dishing up a third portion of ice cream for their unexpected guest, Milo apologized for showing up unannounced saying he'd learned where Dixie lived through their mutual friend Bubba who'd suggested Milo drop in to see her. He hoped Dixie didn't mind.

Dixie said no, she didn't mind, not at all, and why didn't he have a seat at the kitchen table because her living room was piled high with boxes, seeing as she'd moved in only a little over a week ago.

Through his annoyance and from the gist of the small talk between Dixie and Milo, Kyle gathered that unannounced visits were the norm in the rural South, and if you were considered a really good friend, you never entered through the front door, you went to the back. Where Kyle came from, only family was supposed to use the back door. Everyone knew that, or at least they did up north.

"And so," Milo said after finishing his ice cream, "what is it that you do, Kyle?"

Kyle explained the whole farrier thing. Milo had noticed his truck parked outside and was curious about the customizing. "I've got a Dodge Ram 2500 with extended cab myself," Milo volunteered. "It has a heavy-duty Cummins turbo-diesel engine and oversize tars."

At Kyle's puzzled look, Milo explained. "Those things that go on the wheels."

Tires. Kyle still hadn't caught onto the twangy Yewville accent, but it was clear that Milo was making the point that he was a manly man who drove a manly truck. Kyle was willing to give the guy some leeway on the subject, since he himself wasn't remotely interested in the macho aspects of vehicles.

"What do you do?" Kyle asked Milo.

"I've decided to go into business," Milo said. "With new homes going up all around the lake and the retirement village being built between here and Florence, I figure there's a chance to own the biggest plant nursery anywhere around. I learned a lot about the business from my uncle, and he's downsizing now. I figured, hey, why not?"

After that, the conversation thankfully stalled, and Dixie did nothing to jump-start it. Still, Milo tried to drag out the visit by asking questions about virtually every person in their mutual graduating class at Yewville High. Kyle was stifling his third yawn before Milo finally asked Dixie for her phone number and said he had to be going.

"If you need to reach me, you can call me at the office," Dixie said crisply as she whipped a business card out of her pocket. She didn't volunteer her home or cell-phone numbers, and Kyle gave her points for that.

"Yewville Real Estate," Milo said, studying the card. "I was surprised when Priss told me you're selling houses. I thought that you'd be working at the department store in Florence like you did in high school."

"Yes, well, it's a living."

"You sell people the houses, I'll landscape 'em."

Dixie managed a polite smile, yet as Milo was walking toward the door she rolled her eyes for Kyle's benefit, which let Kyle know that she could be—*could be*—as eager for Milo to leave as he was.

With a cheery grin at Dixie and a subdued nod for Kyle, whose presence surely must be the subject of curiosity, Milo edged out the door and loped down the steps toward his truck.

"Whew," Dixie said, closing the door behind him. "I didn't need any of that."

Kyle smiled at her, not stating the obvious: that he didn't, either. The two of them were finally alone, and perhaps they could finally get down to business. First he had to ask the obvious question.

"I gather Milo's recently arrived back in town and that you haven't seen him before this," he said carefully.

"Correct." Outside, Milo's truck started and he threw the engine into Reverse. Through the kitchen window, Kyle caught a glimpse of a bright red finish and fearsome front grille.

Kyle moved closer to Dixie. She seemed like the last person to be impressed by the size of a man's truck. "Dixie, is there anything between you and Milo? Even a little bit of feeling?"

"You've got to be kidding," she said, her voice catching in her throat. For a long moment, they gazed at each other, her mouth opening gradually as if she intended to say something. The manly roar of Milo's pickup receded into the distance, leaving a blessed silence.

The air between them seemed to thicken, grow heavy. Dixie's luminous eyes stared up him with an expression of utter helplessness, which at the moment, was exactly the way Kyle felt, too. He wanted this woman, and he wasn't of a mood to wait. Luckily, as if guided by the same need, she reached for him blindly at the same time as he reached for her, and his arms closed gratefully around her as her lips found his. Soft lips, knowing lips, lips that erased all thought of conventional behavior.

After that, he couldn't have said what hit him. One minute they were merely kissing, then it was as if the Pine Hollow Lake Dam burst, unleashing a flood of passion.

"Dixie," he said unsteadily as she feverishly began to unbutton his shirt, "are you sure you're ready for this?"

Her eyes were solemn but held a glint of merriment. She was enjoying these proceedings, he realized with surprise. Not just accepting and following his lead but playing an active part in his seduction, and all the while, he'd intended to seduce her. The idea amused him so that he chuckled at about the time that she unbuttoned his pants and unzipped the zipper.

Her gaze met his, but her fingers stayed busy. "What's funny about this, Yankee?" she asked lightly.

"I've been planning how to get you in the sack since last night," he said in all honesty.

She laughed. "Would it surprise you if I told you I'd been trying to figure out the same thing? Like how to lure you upstairs to the bedroom without seeming overly forward?"

He nuzzled her throat just below her jawline. "And then what happened? To make you go at me like Pickett's Charge?"

"It was the cherry-vanilla ice cream. Does it every time." She feathered a line of kisses across his chest, her breath hot against his skin.

"Remind me of that later, in case we want to repeat this." He couldn't wait to see her lying back against white sheets, her hair arrayed on the pillow in a shimmer of gold. There would be candles lit in anticipation of a romantic mood, and the scent of lavender rising from the sheets, and all the time in the world to learn about each other's bodies.

But again she surprised him. As they strewed various items of intimate clothing behind them, she led him into a small room off the hall between kitchen and living room.

"Have you ever made love in a sewing room?" she asked without the least bit of coyness.

"No, but I can manage," he replied unsteadily.

"Good, because it takes too long to get upstairs."

The room was furnished with a stack of boxes, miscellaneous items recently unpacked, sewing paraphernalia and a pile of plump quilts in the corner. While he fumbled in his wallet for the necessary packet, she reached down and flicked the quilts into an inviting pile. There was no candlelight and no scent of lavender, but Kyle didn't mind one bit.

When she'd arranged the quilts to her satisfaction, his arms clasped her to him, his hands moving on to explore every fascinating bit of body topography. Breasts, check. Nipples, double-check. Curve of waist, slope of hips, check.

"Kyle." Her voice was low, throaty.

"Mmm," he said, inhaling her scent. It reminded him of wildflowers, of a grassy field after a spring rain. It made him delirious with desire.

"Just. One. Thing."

"What?" *Indeed, what.* What could be so important that Dixie had to talk right now?

"Protection."

"Way ahead of you. I'm on it."

"It's on you is what you mean."

Without wasting a second, holding his gaze with her own, she eagerly pulled him down on top of her and buried her face in his chest as their naked limbs settled into accommodating patterns. His arms tightened around her as he took care to keep his weight balanced on his elbows. With skin pressed against skin, she seemed so delicate, her bones so exquisitely formed, and they fit perfectly together, her curves molding incredibly to his angles.

"I wanted you the first moment I saw you, but I didn't admit it even to myself," she said, her voice muffled softly against his chest.

"I had other things on my mind that day," he said before nibbling gently at the lobe of her ear, pleased at her ensuing sigh of contentment as his lips moved south. Her nipples were dark and rosy in the dim light, and he gently took one in his mouth. It tasted sweet, so sweet, and she moaned with pleasure. His lips explored the slope between her hip bones before making their leisurely way back to her mouth and drawing her into a long, deep kiss. They kissed until he connected with her very soul, felt her total surrender in the way she melted against him.

She was beautiful, the most beautiful woman in the world as he poised above her, hesitating only briefly before entering in one leisurely easeful glide. It was magical, that first moment of warmth and wetness, that experience of becoming one. He settled himself so that their bellies and chests and faces aligned.

"I didn't understand the meaning of Southern hospitality until right now," he whispered close to her ear.

"If Southern women had discovered Yankees could be this much fun, your great-great-great-grandfather's men would have never made it to Savannah on their march to the sea," Dixie said.

"It's a good thing for the Union that they didn't," he said.

"This is the only kind of union I care about," she said with a hint of laughter, and then he found the spot that made her stop talking altogether.

Chapter Four

Sunlight streamed through the curtains that they hadn't closed the night before. Birds outside began to stir up a ruckus. Dixie stretched luxuriously and opened her eyes to find Kyle propped on an elbow, smiling at her.

"Good morning," Kyle said.

"Morning." She closed her eyes, opened them again to make sure she wasn't dreaming. "Did we really do what I think we did last night?"

"More than once."

"Whoa. Whose idea was it?"

"Mine. And yours. Ours." She recalled how they'd adjourned upstairs after their uninhibited spate of lovemaking, neither prepared to call it quits after the first wild rush at each other.

She rolled onto her side so that she was facing him. His hair was endearingly mussed, and his beard was stubbly. He looked great. "Now what?"

"Anything you want," he said. He leaned over and kissed her. He didn't even have morning breath.

"Anything?"

"After last night, I'd hand you the world on a silver platter if it were in my power."

"This is a workday for me," she said regretfully, inscribing a lazy circle on Kyle's chest with one glossily manicured fingernail. "First off I need to call Leland, the man with the Maine coon cats. He plans to make an offer on that house I showed him."

"That's cool," Kyle said.

She swung her legs out of bed. "I wouldn't be getting up right now otherwise." She padded across her bedroom to the bathroom and turned on the shower, looking back over her shoulder. "What's your plan for the day?"

"I'm going to dig up those old bushes cluttering the view of the lake and plant them in a hedge the way you suggested," Kyle called over the noise of the water. She stepped into the shower, then heard the creak of floorboards as he got out of bed. In a moment, his face appeared at the edge of the shower curtain.

"You deserve the day off." Dixie reached for the shampoo, opening her eyes while sudsing her scalp to find Kyle still standing there.

"If you're going to work today, I can, too," he said cheerfully.

"My cousin Jackson owns the garden shop in town. If you need any supplies, that's where to get them. You could go downstairs and start the coffee if you're so inclined. Would you mind?"

"I'm there already. How about breakfast?"

"I'll have time for yogurt," she said. "Blueberry's my favorite."

"I'll top it with granola sprinkles," he said as he headed out the door.

Granola sprinkles? She'd had no idea a man could conceive of such refinements.

Dixie hummed in the shower, pleased that her seduction had worked so well. Or had *he* seduced *her?* Whatever. The occasion had been a spectacular success.

When she arrived downstairs, Kyle handed her a cup of coffee. "I wasn't sure how much sugar or cream, if any," he said. "There are a lot of things I haven't learned about you."

"Yet," she said.

"Maybe we need to talk about that."

"Right now?" She eyed the yogurt, which he'd dumped into one of her favorite bowls, blue with daisies dancing around the rim. Sure enough, he'd sprinkled granola on top.

"Well, later," he conceded.

"Heavy discussion?" She sat down and swirled the yogurt and granola with her spoon.

Kyle rested his fists on the tabletop and smiled at her. "The point is, I hope there will be a later. I'm not eager to go back to Ohio, and last night has something to do with that."

She beamed at him. "That's good. I'd just as soon you'd stick around for a while. At least until you get this yard in shape."

"Agreed." If she looked as besotted as he did right now, he'd get the idea. Which he apparently did, because when she got up to rinse her bowl, Kyle pressed against her from behind.

"I can't wait until you get home," he murmured close to her ear.

"I've got the meeting with the cat man, and I told Mayzelle I'd answer the phones from two o'clock until four," she said, her heartbeat ratcheting up a notch as Kyle rained a series of breathy kisses down the side of her neck. "Then I'll come home and we'll pick up where we left off."

"If we ever left off," he said, kissing her so thoroughly that when they broke apart she had to dash upstairs and repair her lipstick before she could leave.

When she came downstairs again, the fax machine was beeping. She rushed into the small study that she intended to set up as her home office and grabbed an emerging fax. Leland asked to meet her earlier than scheduled; he hadn't been able to reach her on her cell phone last night. Hmm, she wasn't even sure where her cell phone was at the moment. A few minutes spent rooting around under the pile of quilts in the sewing room revealed it, and she stuffed it into her purse. She'd be late if she didn't hurry.

Kyle was outside, digging up a dead rosebush.

"What are you going to do with that?" she asked him.

"Trash heap," he said.

"I don't have a trash heap."

"I started one." He gestured over his shoulder toward the road where he'd piled a bunch of dead tree limbs. He leaned on his shovel and grinned at her, giving her a mental picture of him to hold close throughout the day.

She took care not to show too much thigh as she slid into her Mustang, but could she help it if the breeze caught the edge of her skirt and flounced it nearly to her panty line? Kyle noticed, and his grin widened. She rewarded him with a flirty wave out the open car window.

This unexpected romance was moving fast, Dixie told herself as she gunned the engine down the road toward town at her usual devil-may-care speed. It was unbelievable how involved with Kyle she was already. That could be bad, really bad. Common sense told a person that she should take her time about such things. Find out what kind of man he really was. Decide if he was good for her or not. Figure out whether he was capable of having a healthy relationship.

Somehow that all seemed irrelevant right now. If this should have caused her concern, it didn't. The only thing on her mind was anticipating the next time she and Kyle would be entwined in each other's arms, panting breathlessly and rolling around amid tangled sheets.

KYLE TOOK A BREAK late in the morning and made himself a sandwich. Although Dixie had given him free run of her house, he didn't like to impose. He'd bought a few basic supplies at the supermarket the night before when he'd picked up the ice cream. A loaf of bread, deli items, cans of tuna. He couldn't expect Dixie to take over his care and feeding; he'd always been self-reliant and contributed to the welfare of the women he dated. Women? Make that singular. For a long time, there'd just been Andrea.

Andrea. He should miss her. Only a couple of weeks ago, she'd given him the boot. Since leaving Ohio, his former girlfriend had scarcely crossed his mind. So maybe he didn't love Andrea after all. He wondered, had he ever?

Kyle had met Andrea Ludovici at a neighborhood bar when he'd stopped in for a beer with the guys. He'd found himself sitting next to this tall, thin, emotionally fragile woman who didn't respond to his overtures. She'd stared straight ahead, ordered one drink after another, and by the time they were the only ones still sitting there, she wasn't in any shape to drive herself home.

Naturally, he'd volunteered, and when she started crying after he half carried her to her tiny apartment, it seemed insensitive to leave. So he'd stayed, despite the fact that her barky little Yorkshire terrier bit him on the calf and gloated about it.

They didn't sleep together that night, but Andrea unloaded her misery on him for a good twenty-four hours. She was mourning her previous dog that died, depressed that her mom wouldn't speak to her because of some family snit, and she didn't like working for her boss.

That's how they started up; Kyle had been overcome with pity, Andrea needed a shoulder to cry on. He'd encouraged her to make an appointment with a counselor. He helped her get financing for the accounting firm she wanted to start. He overlooked her abrasive qualities. Though several years older than he, she clung to Kyle so needily that he didn't have the heart to break up with her even when he realized they were totally wrong for each other. He was accustomed to propping people up and making them happy. He'd been doing it all his life, trained to the habit by his father, who, by all accounts, had fallen apart when his wife deserted him and his small son.

Well, why not be nurturing and caring? Helping others gave Kyle great satisfaction. Every once in a while, he'd contemplate what it would be like to date a woman who stood on her own two feet and was proud of it. Where were these women, anyway? He hadn't found any lately.

Since Harry, the colleague covering for him back in Ohio, didn't mind the extra work, Kyle was free to stay on at Dixie's house. He liked getting his hands dirty. There was something elemental about working the earth, and Dixie could use the assistance. The grounds of her house had been neglected for a long time. Kyle thought maybe he'd be happier if he confined his helpfulness to needy plants instead of people. Plants didn't complain that you weren't around to take them to the movies or too busy to go shopping for shoes.

Halfway through moving the bushes, Kyle ran out of the bone meal he poured in the planting holes as nourishment and couldn't finish the job. He considered driving to the garden shop in town to buy more, though with the sky clouding and threatening rain, he probably wouldn't be able to do any more transplanting until the weather cleared. So what to do with himself? Plan future plantings? Figure out what to do about the crumbling rock rim around the pool of the artesian well?

His gaze happened to fall upon the scraps of wood stored near the built-in workbench. He checked them out with the idea of replacing the faulty boards in the dock. A few of the scraps were suitable, and he set them aside.

Kyle had done a bit of tinkering in his time, creating fancy birdhouses alongside his father in his youth. Those birdhouses had been unique, no two alike. Rummaging in the scrap bin, he found everything he needed to build a birdhouse to hang from the branches of the old oak down by the picnic table.

He started to work, eager to surprise Dixie. This house wasn't the fanciest he'd ever made, but birds didn't care. As he was threading a cord through the screw eye he'd attached for hanging, Dixie drove up. She noticed the light over the workbench as soon as she got out of the car. "What have you been up to?" she asked, craning over his shoulder while he kissed her cheek.

"Just frittering time," he said, inhaling her scent. She was the most sensationally feminine woman he'd ever met in his life.

She studied his handiwork with all its embellishments—a strip of elaborate carved molding on the edge of the roof, a tiny porch to shelter the perch. "Why, Kyle," she said slowly and with amazement, "what a lovely thing you've made."

"It's nothing," he said.

She eyed him and frowned. "Misplaced humility doesn't become you," she said with mock sternness.

"I haven't finished it yet. It needs painting."

"We have lots of paint. The previous owners meant to fix the place up before they put it on the market but never got around to it." She reached for a can of enamel. "Here's a nice yellow. We have royal blue, fern green, bubble-gum pink and white, of course. Take your pick."

"How about basic white?" Kyle suggested, beyond his depth when any decorating was involved.

"Too unimaginative. How about pink with white trim and a green roof?"

"That's okay with me."

Dixie beamed. "Where will we be hanging this, Kyle?"

"Over the picnic table, so the birds will have a nice lake view," he said.

She laughed. "By the way, Leland Porter, the Maine coon man, is buying the house I showed him, and he wants to give me a cat."

"A cat would make it lively around here. The birds would have to mind their p's and q's."

"I've always been more into dogs than cats. Taking them for walks in freezing-cold temperatures, throwing a slobbery ball for them to catch, coming home to find a shredded couch pillow strewn all over the living room—it all sounds like such fun."

"You're weird, Dixie. Listen, cats are great. They purr."

She smiled. "Good point. Now, about dinner—veal parmesan?"

"Fantastic," Kyle said.

He helped her carry grocery bags into the house and watched while she stowed the contents in the pantry. "Anything I can do to help?"

She stood on tiptoe and planted a kiss on his cheek. "Paint the birdhouse. I can't wait to see how pretty it will be."

Whistling, Kyle headed back to the garage. Outside, dusk was settling in, and in the watery sunlight filtering through the cloud cover, a fine mist sparkled on the newly transplanted bushes. As he pried open paint cans, a mantle of contentment settled over him, a new and unexpected state of being. He stopped what he was doing and savored it for a long moment, wondering if this was what other people experienced in their lives. He'd like to preserve it, make it last.

In order to do that, he probably needed to figure out what had caused this feeling of well-being in the first place. It seemed way too simplistic to credit Dixie. Surely this new relationship couldn't be responsible for such a quick change in his level of satisfaction.

He started to paint the birdhouse, embellishing it with little curlicues around the perch. Dixie wouldn't expect him to be that original, he figured. And it was fun to surprise her. It made him feel good just to see her smile.

THOUGH NEITHER OF THEM commented about a future together, Kyle and Dixie settled into a routine of sorts. He worked in her yard and repaired the dock. She went to the office. He helped her make sense out of a tangle of fax machine and computer cords so she could set up her home office in the small den.

"Why don't you bring your laptop in here," she suggested. "It must be hard to run a business out of your truck."

He appreciated having an orderly place to work and began to have his business calls forwarded to Dixie's landline, which he used to communicate with Harry back in Ohio. He placed orders for supplies from his computer and corresponded with customers through e-mail.

Sometimes he and Dixie unpacked boxes together so she could put things away. She'd inherited a lot of family heirlooms. Old lace, photos, an oak high chair that converted into a rocking chair. Dixie used the high chair as a plant stand and framed lace fragments to hang in the dining room. She dragged out a bunch of photo albums and lined the staircase wall with pictures of her family.

"That's Granddaddy and Memaw Frances," she said, pointing to an old black-and-white photograph of a young couple posed in wedding finery. She moved on to another picture of a sweet-faced young woman wearing a white-collared blue dress. "This is Miss Alma, Daddy's first wife who died young. I never met her, of course, because he didn't marry my mom until later, and then they had two kids, Carrie and me. Here's Rabun, Daddy's son with Miss Alma. Rabun went away when I was a child, so I never really knew him all that well. And this is Mama when she won a first-place ribbon at the county fair for her corn relish. Oh, and here's Carrie and Luke at their wedding."

All these people—who they were and what they'd accomplished with their lives—gave him insight into Dixie, helped him understand what made her tick. As far as he could figure out, it was family, friends and religion. Compared to hers, his own life was beginning to seem sterile and unfocused. Dixie was a window into a different world, one that fascinated him with its many elements.

When she arrived home in the evening, Dixie prepared dinner. She cooked things a man could savor—meat with gravy, most vegetables fresh. They ate collards seasoned with fatback. They rolled dumplings on her wide kitchen counter. Some mornings she made light, flaky biscuits, and he devoured them with country ham, eggs, grits and red-eye gravy. She always kept a pitcher of sweet iced tea in the refrigerator, and he grew accustomed to pouring himself a glass a few times a day. He learned to like Cheerwine, the Carolinas' soft drink of choice.

At night, the two of them cuddled in her bed while they watched old movies on DVD. They stocked potato chips in a dresser drawer so they wouldn't have to interrupt their movie watching to go downstairs and get a snack. Still, they made good use of the pause button when their own love scenes became more intense than those onscreen.

Life was romantic. Kyle felt a flutter in his stomach whenever he saw Dixie walking across a room, and when he first set eyes on her after a day of being apart, his heart did a little hippety-hop. They held hands when they walked together, and his arm found its way around her shoulders when they rode in his truck. Theirs was a sensual relationship. They got along well, too. It was a happy house.

Sometimes Kyle had to remind himself that Dixie had just moved in to a new place and that the atmosphere of good cheer prevailed in spite of various hardships that had to be endured. The plumbing, for instance. When he discovered that the hot-water faucet in the downstairs half bath didn't work, he repaired it and surprised Dixie when she came home from work by blindfolding her, leading her to the sink, turning on the tap and guiding her hand under the stream.

"What is this supposed to be, a Helen Keller moment?" she joked, referring to the famous scene in the movie where Helen's teacher, Anna Sullivan, held Helen's hand under a water pump to drive home the point that words had connections to real things. Kyle turned up the hot water, and as the warm water increased, Dixie got it. She responded by pulling off the blindfold, throwing her arms around him and giving him a big kiss.

"Hey," he protested. "It was no big deal."

She became all serious and he could have sworn she had tears in her eyes. "It is to me," she told him quietly.

Little things he did made her happy. He liked that. He began to understand that even though Dixie was independent and could do almost anything she set her mind to, she appreciated his help.

"I've never had a man in my life who took care of me. Not since Daddy and Granddaddy," she said.

You do now, he wanted to say, though he was too new to this whole business to say it flat out.

Together they repainted the living room, which the previous owners, for some unfathomable reason, had painted bathtub-ring gray. Dixie chose a soft shade of yellow, as pale as cream, and once it was done, they exchanged an exuberant high five.

"Another house sale, and I'll be able to buy a couple of chairs," Dixie said. Except for the couch, she'd ditched her living-room set when she moved. "It was time to make room for new things," she told him.

"As long as I'm one of them," Kyle said, and she laughed and hugged him. He liked spontaneous displays of affection. His life had been devoid of them for so long that they always took him by surprise.

Kyle kept busy. So far he'd assembled five more bird-houses and promised another to Mayzelle, whom he'd met when he stopped by the real estate office one day. Dixie chose the colors for the birdhouses, and he considered them gaudy. Dixie was so certain of her choices that he went ahead and painted them as she suggested. He had to admit they were cute.

"Why, I declare, this is the most adorable birdhouse I've ever seen in my life," Mayzelle said to him when he deliv-ered it. "You could sell these at the flea market."

"I build them for fun, not for profit," Kyle said.

Dixie was almost as enthusiastic about the flea-market venture as Mayzelle. "Let's take a few on Saturday and try to sell them," she suggested. "At the same time, I'll unload the bric-a-brac that the previous owners left in my house."

She seemed to be anticipating this enterprise with so much pleasure that Kyle didn't have the heart to deny her. When Sat-urday arrived, Kyle would just as soon have stayed in bed, but Dixie coaxed him out from under the covers before it was fully light. Together they loaded his truck with baskets of junk, old clothes and the birdhouses, which now numbered seven.

"Where's this flea market?" Kyle asked. Even the sight of Dixie all dewy from her shower didn't quite make up for leaving so early.

"We'll hang a left at the nuclear plant onto the Allentown Road. It's a five-mile drive to the old tobacco-market shed where they hold the flea market. Carrie and I used to go once and a while and get rid of old household items."

"Are you sure anyone will be interested in birdhouses?" he asked skeptically.

"Of course. They're wonderfully imaginative. I love the one with the front porch and rocking chair."

"Speaking of porches, did I mention that I'm going to show the Meehan house next week? My client's name is Lana Pillsbry, she's a teacher at Yewville Elementary. She's been in the house before and likes it. I hope I can get her to sign on the dotted line before we ever leave the property."

Kyle grinned. "You're a real go-getter, Dixie."

"Daddy brought Carrie and me up that way. If he'd lived long enough, he would have been proud of how well we've done in our chosen professions." She paused, a habit of hers before changing the subject. "How did you become a farrier, Kyle?"

He kept his eyes focused on the road ahead. "I graduated from college with a degree in history. My only job offer involved flipping burgers. Shoeing horses seemed more lucrative, and the area needed farriers."

"How'd you learn it?"

"In my senior year I had a job exercising horses at a local stable, and the guy who shoed the horses liked me. He trained a student or two every year and asked me if I wanted to learn to be a farrier. It was the best thing I ever did."

He braked at a sign that said Flea Market and turned into the parking lot. As he parked the truck, he slid his arm around the back of the seat. Could he help it that Dixie was so delectably and unconsciously seductive? He kept going, closing the distance between them. It was only a few inches to the clean line of her jaw, the soft skin of her throat.

"Don't ruin my lipstick again," she warned. "I didn't bring any with me."

"You're fine without it," he said, ruining her lipstick anyway. He came up for air. "Did you wear a bra?"

"Yes."

"No," he retorted as he lifted her shirt.

"I lied." Invitingly, she slid down in the seat.

This was what he liked about this woman. "Dixie, have you ever made love in the front seat of a farrier's truck?"

"No," she whispered, "but I'm ready to prove it can be done."

It was a while before they unloaded the truck, and before they did, they came close to scandalizing a few old biddies parking nearby.

FLEA-MARKET BUSINESS was brisk right from the start. As they set up their booth, Dixie self-consciously avoided Kyle's eyes. Every time their gaze met, they both began to sputter with laughter.

"And what is the price for this one?" a mother asked him after her young daughter dragged her over to the booth where he and Dixie were displaying their wares.

Off the top of his head, Kyle named a dollar figure for the birdhouse, and the mother shelled out her money along with the comment that she wasn't going to hang this wonderful creation outside where the elements might work their way with it. No, this was too special, and little Chelsea demanded that it occupy the dresser in her room.

As soon as the woman and her daughter walked off, a woman with a behind the size of a cement mixer swooped down upon Dixie. "Why, Dixie Lee! I haven't seen you since your sister's wedding!"

"Hello, Mrs. Hatcher. How have you been?" Dixie smiled politely, clueing Kyle in to the fact that she didn't really like the woman very much.

"Why, I've been fine, though I sure do miss Carrie at the gas station. That Hub is a nice fellow, but he doesn't have the gift of gab."

"I'm sure Hub gives the customers good service," Dixie replied.

"I've been hearing about you and your new boyfriend," Mrs. Hatcher said, wagging her forefinger. Her tight yellow curls bobbed up and down with each wag.

"Um, Mrs. Hatcher, this is Kyle Sherman," Dixie said, drawing Kyle forward.

"You won't find a nicer girl than our Dixie here," Mrs. Hatcher said, looking him over before she turned back to Dixie. "Dear, Milo told Priss he'd seen you since he moved back home." She aimed a sly sideways glance at Kyle. He stared back with what he hoped was a blank expression.

"Yes, Milo stopped by to visit with Kyle and me one evening," Dixie replied coolly.

"Hmm, I didn't realize you and he stayed in touch," Mrs. Hatcher said, her forehead puckering.

"We didn't, but Priss and I were friends long before Milo and I knew each other," Dixie pointed out.

"Naturally she'd keep you posted," Mrs. Hatcher said, obviously fishing for more information.

"Have you noticed these birdhouses that Kyle makes?" Dixie asked, refusing to swallow the bait. She guided Mrs. Hatcher toward them.

Kyle, amused at Dixie's adroit handling of the situation, stood back as Dixie pointed out the unusual features of the ones remaining. No wonder she was doing so well selling real estate, he reflected. She was adept at focusing a buyer's attention, and she kept working at it until she'd clinched the sale. This meant that Mrs. Hatcher eventually churned down the aisle with two birdhouses under her arm, safely distracted from Dixie's love life.

Dixie collapsed against him. "That woman freaks me out. She's so nosy."

"About Milo, you mean?"

"About everything. She's not all that unusual. Around here there's not all that much to do." Dixie spoke ruefully, as if she wished she could change that facet of small-town life but realized it was pointless to try.

He studied her expression for a long moment. "Dixie, does it worry you that people talk about us?"

"Not exactly. They'd gossip in the same way if I *didn't* date. In fact, that's what happened last year. People kept asking when I was going to find a new boyfriend. In a way, they were just being friendly. I keep getting phone calls from people who'd like to set me up with a brother over in Timmonsville or a forty-year-old cousin who's never married."

"Now you have me." Kyle pulled her behind the concrete pillar, drawing her into a full-body hug. Dixie giggled, a sound like a purling brook, and they remained in an embrace until someone walked up to the booth.

In the next few hours, he and Dixie sold all the birdhouses and took orders for more. Kyle was astonished at their success.

In the afternoon, as crowds began to disperse, they closed the booth and loaded their unsold items into the truck. Out of habit, Kyle opened his cell phone before he started the engine. They were in range of a tower, and he quickly checked his messages. One from Elliott. One from his landlady, Mrs. Steidel, reporting she'd watered the dracaena. And two from Andrea. He frowned and snapped the phone shut.

On the drive back toward Yewville, Dixie counted out his share of the money and folded it into an old breath-mint tin in his glove compartment.

"I kind of have the urge to splurge with this windfall," he told her. "Would it be enough for a down payment on one of your listings?"

"Doubtful," she said with a little laugh.

"I'm not sure you took me seriously when I mentioned it. Really, I mean to check out some properties."

A long pause, almost too long. "If you're sure you want to…" Dixie let her sentence taper off as if waiting for reassurance.

"It's an option," he said, considering that it had only recently become one and that perhaps he shouldn't trust his gut feelings on this.

Before he could waver, Dixie rose to the challenge. "How about now?" she asked.

"You're serious?"

"Try me."

"Okay, turn right at the next stop sign."

"Really?"

"Yes, really."

Dixie directed him to a small frame house with an attached garage. He liked the garage—it provided lots of space where he could store the tools of his trade—but the house was a disaster. Someone had altered the original three-bedroom, two-bath floor plan by chopping it into smaller spaces. It now had five minuscule bedrooms and hardly any living room.

"This won't work for me," Kyle said, though he did like the location. By his reckoning, it wasn't far from Dixie's place.

As they walked back to the truck, it occurred to Kyle that he had no idea whether or not he would feel comfortable moving to the South. He could be viewing home ownership as nothing more than a way to stay close to Dixie. Which didn't seem like a bad idea as they drove home beneath big trees shading the road, their shadows growing longer as the sun slid toward the horizon. That elusive feeling of contentment wormed its way into his consciousness again, and he rested a hand on Dixie's knee. This stage of getting to know each other seemed idyllic, perfect and almost too good to be true.

By the time they reached the bypass around Yewville, Kyle was happily anticipating spending a cozy evening together. "What do you say we stop off and pick up a couple of steaks at Bi-Lo?" he suggested. "I could grill them outside."

Dixie responded with enthusiasm. "Yes! I'll throw together a salad and we'll bake potatoes."

Kyle was on the verge of asking what wine she'd like to drink with dinner. Before he could form the words, his cell phone rang.

His mind still on the wine, Kyle reached into the cubbyhole next to the glove compartment for the phone. When he glanced at the caller ID, he all but groaned. "Oh, great. It's my ex-girlfriend." The words slipped out before he even thought.

Dixie stared at him, her eyes wide. At that moment, Kyle regretted to the depths of his soul that he'd never seen fit to tell Dixie about Andrea. He had the disconcerting feeling that he'd made a huge mistake, but continuing to ignore Andrea's calls would only compound it. He knew from experience that she wouldn't give up until he either answered or called her back.

With Dixie glaring at him accusingly and his heart sinking, he opened the phone and said, "Hello?"

Chapter Five

Out on Pine Hollow Lake, someone was fishing from a row-boat. A noisy flock of geese landed, kicking up a spray of water nearby, and a trail of white vapor from the power plant faded into the darkening sky. Dixie and Kyle sat at the picnic table near the playhouse, where Dixie busied herself tearing apart bits of pine straw littering the top of it. She was still incredulous that Kyle had a girlfriend that he'd never mentioned. *Ex*-girlfriend, he swore. If that was the case, why then was the woman calling him?

Kyle finally spoke. "Her name is Andrea," he said heavily.

"I gathered that." Dixie picked up a new pine needle to trash and broke it into little segments.

"Andrea and I split before I left for the reenactment at Rivervale Bridge," he said. "She even took her toothbrush back to her own apartment. She never did that when we broke up before."

"Oh, well, taking her toothbrush, that's pretty final," Dixie said, keeping her spine ramrod stiff. She lifted her eyes to his. "How many times have you broken up and gone back together?"

"Four or five. I'm telling you, Dixie, it's over. I told Andrea the same thing a few minutes ago. And you heard me."

"She sounded as if she didn't believe it," Dixie pointed out. "She sounded hot on your trail." Maybe *hot* was a word she'd have been better off not using.

"I left Ohio three weeks ago and haven't called her, haven't sent her a postcard, haven't e-mailed. She was trying to find out if I was going to the reenactment of the battle of New Market, Virginia, in May. In his message my friend Elliott said he has been having trouble reaching me on my cell phone."

"Maybe you need another phone plan," Dixie said helpfully. "So you can stay in touch with all your old friends." She couldn't quite keep the bite of sarcasm out of her tone.

"I don't care about any of them right now," Kyle said, his eyes somber and begging for understanding. "All I care about is you."

If they hadn't been sitting across a table from each other discussing this sanely and rationally, there was every indication that he might have taken her in his arms. She wished he would, but first she needed to find out more about this Andrea person.

"I'm so disappointed, Kyle. I thought we were being upfront with each other. You knew about Milo. And I've mentioned other guys to let you know I have something of a past but no one in my present." Considering the spirit of openness that she thought characterized their relationship, she was bewildered that Kyle had kept her in the dark. Maybe being open and honest was an aspect of small-town life. Maybe the fact that everyone knew everything about you got things out faster, more easily, because if you didn't tell all, someone else would. And usually not with the same slant.

"Like I said, it's over. She took her toothbrush and her dog and—"

"She has a dog?"

"A yappy little Yorkie named Twinkle. She carries him around in her purse."

Dixie was of the opinion that if a person was going to have a dog, it shouldn't be a fashion accessory. A dog should run around getting muddy in streams, shaking water on the carpet, terrorizing squirrels. However, that was a personal choice, and besides, she suspected that she was soon going to be transformed into a cat person.

"No wonder you broke up a lot."

"It wasn't just the dog. I didn't have a whole lot of patience with her temper. Or the way she liked to boss me around."

"What didn't she have patience for?"

"My truck. My hobby. My clothes, my friends, my work. Horse manure on my boots."

"In other words, everything that didn't have to do with her. Unless the horse manure…"

"She hates it. Thinks horses are nasty creatures. She tried to smooth away all my rough edges, and I stopped letting her. I yam what I yam, like Popeye."

Dixie shrugged. "Too bad she didn't get the picture before you'd invested all that time in this nonrelationship. How long were you a couple, Kyle?"

"About five years, more or less."

"She'd like to go for six, right?"

"She probably saw a piece of jewelry she likes and figures that if she can manipulate me so I feel guilty, I'll buy it for her as an act of contrition."

"Is that what you do to make up? Buy her jewelry?"

"I never bought her the piece that really counts. I never sprang for the engagement ring."

This was way too much to absorb. "I'm going in the house," she said.

"We didn't stop to buy the steaks. How about if we order Chinese food? There aren't too many problems that crispy duck won't fix." The offer sounded desperate.

"There's no Chinese unless we go to Florence."

"Oh." He looked crestfallen.

Dixie regretted not having a Chinese restaurant nearby. She could use a fortune cookie right now, especially if it offered advice on where they should go from here.

She heaved a giant sigh. "Kyle, I need time out from all this. From *us*. I have to think about things."

"You're entitled," he said evenly. He eyed her with something akin to humor. "Want me to come inside and get my toothbrush?"

"I noticed that you have another one in the playhouse. The brush with Doc Johnson's name on it."

"Okay. That's fair enough. Dixie, this—this pains me. And I swear, there's nothing between Andrea and me anymore. I swear it." He stood, turned on his heel and strode off, hands in his pockets, a forlorn slump to his shoulders.

Dixie sat at the picnic table long after he'd gone inside. She imagined Kyle bumping his head on the rafters, showering in the small cubicle. She pictured him lowering himself onto the narrow cot. Of course he was naked, which was the way he always slept. Of course her imagination gave him a pillow to hug instead of her.

It was more than she could stand. She wrapped her arms around herself against the chill fog creeping across the lake and hurried inside the house to her own bed, which was just as lonely as his.

MAYZELLE WAS ASTONISHED when Dixie confided that she and Kyle were on the outs. Mayzelle had liked Kyle the few times they'd met. She evinced her surprise in a series of pertinent questions.

"You never heard of this Andrea person before she called on his phone?" Mayzelle asked skeptically. She sat at her desk across from Dixie at the real estate office and gave up all pretense of doing any work, which this morning was supposed to consist of printing out the contract for Dixie's recent sale to the Maine coon man.

"If Kyle didn't see fit to tell me about her, how would I?" Dixie retorted. She pulled out her PDA and checked the day's schedule. She was due at a chamber of commerce coffee in twenty minutes, and later, she'd take Lana to tour the house she liked. After that, nothing to do and nowhere to go except home, where Kyle was probably planting bulbs along the front sidewalk. They hadn't spoken yesterday, and she'd gone off and left him on his own, while she attended the regular Sunday family dinner.

Mayzelle was not about to quit. She pursed her plump cheeks and tilted her head to the side. "Are you and Kyle going to break up, Dixie? Or have you already?"

Dixie sighed. "I'm bummed out because he never saw fit to mention a recent ex-girlfriend, whereas I made sure I revealed everything about me and my exes. Andrea called. He answered the phone, and he wouldn't have had to, since her name popped up on the caller ID and he knew very well who it was."

"Then what?"

"Kyle did seem put out about her calling, though that could've been because he was peeved that she'd called when

I was in the truck with him. They could have talked before. Recently. Often."

Mayzelle waved away this possibility with a flip of her bejeweled hand. "I don't think you should get all bent out of shape over this. You said Kyle's cell phone doesn't work in Yewville. How would Andrea reach him? How would he call her? There's no phone in that playhouse of yours, is there?"

"No, but he's around my house all day. He could have been carrying on conversations with Andrea on the landline while I'm at work. Maybe they were e-mailing."

"You're a bit too suspicious, Dixie. Like someone who isn't very sure of herself? Like a person who isn't confident that she's all her man could want?"

Mayzelle was only trying to be helpful, but Dixie dismissed the idea of self-esteem problems. "That's not it."

"What I do when I'm trying to solve a problem," said Mayzelle, "is make a list of pros and cons. What do you like about Kyle? What are his good points?"

His performance in bed, Dixie thought right away. She couldn't bring herself to say it out loud, though.

"He keeps his underwear picked up," she said.

"What else?"

"He never forgets to sprinkle granola on my breakfast yogurt. And we really get along well. He encourages me and likes me and makes me think I'd like to spend the rest of my life with him," she finished, all in a rush.

"Oh. Well. Maybe you're making a molehill out of a mountain over this ex-girlfriend of his."

"You've got it backward, Mayzelle. Mountain out of a molehill." Dixie had to laugh, in spite of herself.

Mayzelle recovered admirably. "Of course. And speaking

of molehills, I need to run by the garden center and ask your cousin Jackson what to do about pests. Moles nearly drove us crazy last summer tunneling all over the place, and I suspect I've got aphids on my aspidistras." Mayzelle nudged her poodle awake with one foot and snapped the leash onto the dog's collar. "Come on, Fluffy, let's go." To Dixie she said, "You've got some deciding to do, girl."

"I'll think about that tomorrow, like Scarlett O'Hara," Dixie said, making a face.

"You be careful, or it's Kyle who will be gone with the wind," Mayzelle cautioned. She tripped past Dixie's desk, Fluffy leading the way with her own peculiar waddle.

"Why is my life so difficult?" Dixie said to Mayzelle's retreating back. She suddenly remembered something. "Mayzelle, while you're at the garden center, ask Jackson to drop off a couple of bags of mulch on his way home tonight." Kyle intended to spread it around the azaleas.

This caught Dixie up short. If she and Kyle parted ways, he'd be heading back to Ohio soon. The azaleas wouldn't get mulched, and she'd have to go back to her previous lonely way of life. Heck, she'd have to start remembering to sprinkle granola on her own yogurt.

Which brought her back to the central issue: Did she really want Kyle to go away? And wouldn't a permanent rift drive him right back into Andrea's arms?

"You know, Mayzelle," Dixie said slowly, "I don't believe I will break up with Kyle over this."

Mayzelle stopped walking halfway to the door and turned around. Fluffy did, too.

"Smart girl," Mayzelle said approvingly.

IN THE SPIRIT of reconciliation, Dixie was waiting for Kyle in the playhouse that evening when he came in from building birdhouses in the garage. She'd parked her car behind a clump of bushes down the road and walked home, taking care that Kyle couldn't observe her through the garage window.

Kyle took his time about showing up, which only made Dixie more eager. Before entering the shadowy interior, he stomped his feet free of dirt on the slab of bluestone outside the door. Once inside, he proceeded to unbutton his shirt much too slowly for her expectations and untucked it from his jeans. These were cramped quarters, and his view of her in bed was blocked by the hanging light fixture suspended from the low ceiling. Dixie scarcely dared to breathe; she intended for Kyle to spot her unawares, wanted to watch color suffuse his face when he realized what she had in mind.

By the time he bent to untie his shoelaces, she was almost out of air. And then as he straightened, which was not really straightening because the ceiling required that he stoop, he saw her.

"Hey, Kyle, have you ever made love in a Hobbit house before?"

He stared back as if she were an apparition. For a long unbearable moment, she considered that this had been a terrible mistake. Maybe there was nothing between them, had never been anything but her own sexual hankerings.

"I think it can be managed," he said.

He held her gaze and she began to feel the powerful stirrings that had become so commonplace when they were together. Her chest tightened with emotion. Everything between them up until this point flashed through her mind in fast-forward mode—her first sight of him in his Yankee uniform, the quiet breakfast the day after he arrived, his dark shape looming over her in the small sewing room where they'd made love the first time.

It was easy after that. All she did was open her arms to him. Her breath seemed to stop in her throat, and she clasped him to her, her hands tight against the muscles of his back. Above her, he was a vague outline in the half dark, and she moaned as he lowered his face to her throat. His lips teased her, and then his teeth, and she threw her head back so he would have better access.

He still had too many clothes on. She tugged at his waistband, somehow pushed the fabric out of the way, and then the briefs underneath. When Dixie would have grasped him and pulled him closer, he seized her hands and pinned them above her head.

Then he settled over her again and let his weight bear down upon her so strongly that she couldn't move. He began to pump slowly, so slowly that she could barely feel it. Her instinct was to arch her back and push against him, but he was heavy and all she could do was lie back and enjoy each delectable movement.

She could not think of anything else except his strong, hard body moving against hers. And she gave freely, knowing nothing else, being no one else. In those minutes that she stretched into eternity, she was his. And he, more than any other time before, was hers.

How he managed to contain himself as long as he did was an amazement to her, since this way of lovemaking was exquisite torture. When she felt his increase in excitement, understood that he had reached that point of inner concentration where the outcome was assured, they matched each other move for move, two halves of the same whole.

Dixie had never merged her spirit with a man like this, had never known that exact white-hot heat throbbing from her core, and had most certainly never felt the oneness that she experienced afterward as they lay side by side, exhausted and complete. As she spiraled down from that incredible high, she caressed Kyle's chest with delicate fingers, marveling at the wondrous complexities of their mating.

"Dixie," he said. "Oh, Dixie. We shouldn't let unimportant things come between us."

"I don't care about Andrea," she said fiercely. "She really doesn't bother me at all." It was true. Making love with each other had vanquished all old relationships, hers and his.

"That's exactly how I feel," Kyle said, and while she was preparing for further discussion that would define their relationship once and for all, he fell asleep in her arms.

Dixie smiled tenderly to herself. It was, after all, a discussion they could have anytime. She was secure in the knowledge that they'd covered a whole lot of ground in the past few weeks. They'd dreamed together, they'd misunderstood each other. They'd fought and made up. Declaring their feelings out loud could wait.

"I GUESS WE MIGHT be ready for those steaks that we never had," Kyle said when they woke up. It was dark outside now, and she was cradled against his shoulder, their bodies tight against each other because of the restrictions of the small bed.

"Steaks?" Dixie asked.

"I went to the store and bought them today just in case," he said.

She raised herself on an elbow and gazed at him. "Overly optimistic, weren't you?" she asked playfully. "Considering how things were going between us yesterday."

Kyle shook his head. "I was sure we wouldn't continue on. All day it was as if—as if some vital part of me had been torn away."

"Me, too," she said softly. She laid her head back on his shoulder. "We've grown so close. At first, it seemed that we were moving too fast. Now, well, maybe it would be too fast with another person but not with you. Do you understand what I'm saying?"

"Yes, I do," he said, a note of wonder creeping into his tone. He kissed her on the forehead. "We need to allow ourselves to be swept away. Otherwise—" He stopped, seeming to assess her reaction. "Otherwise, we're not fully living in the experience." His arms tightened around her. "We had an affinity from the beginning. As soon as I met you, I already understood things about you that would take a long time to learn about someone else."

"We can be who we really are with each other. That's important."

"Very. And who I am is really hungry."

She smiled, then sat up, or tried to. Instead she fell to the floor, forced out of the narrow bed at a most inopportune time.

Kyle grabbed for her but missed, and fortunately the cot was low, only a foot or so high. She landed gently, and before she knew it, he had rolled out beside her and was kneeling before her. He took her face in his hands, kissed her with unmistakable emotion, drawing her close.

"Sweet Dixie," he said in the most heartfelt way imaginable. "I'm crazy about you."

She was more than crazy about him but willed herself to be patient while they grew together into what she hoped would be a new life for both of them. Hadn't Kyle said that it was important for a couple to grow within the relationship? There was nothing she desired more, and she was determined to make that happen however she could. Kyle Sherman was a man worth waiting for.

They cooked the steaks on the outside grill and served them with a fresh green salad. It was warm enough to take their desserts outside and sit on the back steps to eat them.

"How did you know I love cherry cobbler?" Kyle said, digging into it with gusto.

"You like cherry-vanilla ice cream," she pointed out, recalling the night when he'd made a special trip to the supermarket to buy it.

"I like cherry pie, too," he said. "I stopped in at the Eat Right for some the other day."

"Kathy Lou told me," Dixie said.

"Kathy Lou," Kyle said with a certain amount of resignation. "The Yewville town gossip."

"She's not any worse than anyone else."

"I can't do squat without someone telling you about it," Kyle said.

Dixie smiled. "It works both ways."

"I don't mind. I have no intention of doing anything I can't share with you."

She set aside her dish of cobbler. "Have you ever made love on top of a picnic table?" she asked.

He started to laugh. "Honey, you're going to kill me with all this good lovin'."

"Is that a yes or a no?"

"I could be talked into it. What about all these little acorns on the tabletop I noticed this morning?"

"You get a whisk broom and I'll bring a blanket," she said, and she heard Kyle's laughter following her as she headed to the linen closet.

DIXIE'S FRIEND Joyanne showed up for a brief visit toward the end of the week and stopped by the real estate office to ask Dixie if she was free for lunch. These days, Joyanne preferred to be called Joy since she'd changed her name and gone Hollywood. Joy's new life sounded exciting, especially now that she'd signed on for the part of a pioneer schoolteacher in a new TV drama.

"We're going to start rehearsing in a couple of weeks," Joy said. "Once we're in production, I won't get a chance to visit down home for a while. You have to promise to come to California soon, Dixie. I'm going to be moving out of my apartment, and then I won't have all that much contact with the guy upstairs. Remember, the Arnold Schwarzenegger clone? Plus, his name is slightly easier to spell than Schwarzenegger."

"What is his name, anyway?" Dixie might as well show some interest in Joy's new life.

"It's Zeb Chance," Joy said. "Plus, he's better-looking than Arnold. At least in my opinion."

"What kind of name is Zeb Chance?" Dixie asked, fascinated by this penchant of Hollywood types to change their names.

"A made-up one. He's worked in a couple of movies as a stuntman, but his true passion is directing."

"Why don't you go out with him?"

"Not my type. Wow, your teeth look great. So does your permanent eyeliner." Joy stared for a moment.

"I had to go to Florence to get the eyeliner done. I'm glad you like it." Dixie took a pocket mirror out of her middle desk drawer and studied her reflection.

"Anyway, looking the way you do must attract guys in huge numbers. Maybe you don't have a need to meet Zeb Chance. Though you did state that it's your intention to find a suitable spouse ASAP."

"I merely stated that I want what most of our girlfriends have by now, a husband and pictures of our kids plastered all over the refrigerator. Acquiring a man is one of my priorities like it is with everyone else. I admit it, that's all."

"Any new contenders?"

Dixie contemplated her manicure. "I've found a guy I like a lot. I hope you'll get a chance to meet him."

"You mean, this Kyle that everyone's talking about? Is he husband material?"

"Maybe, and how did you hear about him? More to the point, *what* did you hear?"

"My mom mentioned him last week. She says the two of you are inseparable."

"How'd she find that out?"

"At the Eat Right, I guess. Also, I ran into Priss at the airport. She said Milo told her about Kyle."

"Milo only met Kyle once."

Joy's eyebrows raised at that. "How?"

Dixie explained about Milo's dropping in. She didn't mention her adventures with Kyle on the sewing-room floor as soon as Milo left.

Joy listened with interest. "Milo told Priss to ask you over sometime so he can see you without Kyle. I guess Kyle's a permanent fixture by now, huh?"

"I'd like him to be," Dixie admitted. "He's talking about moving here from Ohio."

Joy laughed. "You're in the right business to facilitate that." She waved at the home brochures stacked in the cubbyholes above Dixie's desk.

"I've only shown Kyle houses I'm sure he won't like," Dixie said. "We went to look at another one yesterday. It had a loft reachable only from outside, and one of the two bathrooms had no toilet. I was positive he'd hate it."

"What's the point, exactly?"

"The longer I take to find Kyle a suitable home, the longer he'll live in my playhouse."

"Dixie! You're shameless! Anyway, unless he's a midget, that tiny little place must cramp his style. And a few other things besides."

Dixie managed a sheepish grin. "Kyle's not really living there anymore, Joyanne."

"Joy," her friend corrected automatically.

"Sorry. It's hard to remember."

"That's okay, I understand. So the man has moved into your house?"

"Most of his clothes now occupy the extra closet in my bedroom. I hope you're not shocked."

Joy made a face at this. "After living in Hollywood, nothing shocks me anymore. I'm glad you've found someone, Dixie. You deserve the best."

"Kyle is…well, he's wonderful. A real keeper. Oh, Mayzelle's driving up in front, so we can leave for lunch in a few minutes. I'll tell you all about it over banana splits at the Eat Right."

"I'll have to order a fruit plate. My diet, remember?"

They had been eating banana splits for lunch a couple of times a month since they were thirteen, and Dixie hated to give up that tradition. Still, she understood that they'd both moved on in their lives, were learning new things, becoming attached to new people.

"All right, I'll have the fruit plate, too," Dixie said with a sigh. "As long as you promise me you'll come over for dinner tonight, I'll forgive you about the banana split. I can't wait for you to meet Kyle. He's everything I ever hoped for in a man. Handsome, charming, smart, sexy—"

"Glad about the sexy," Joy said, rolling her eyes.

Dixie grinned. "You'll like Kyle, I'm sure you will." Like a kid with a new toy, she could hardly wait to show him off. Once she'd met Kyle, let Joyanne—Joy—tell Dixie that she needed to meet this Zeb Chance. Dixie was sure he couldn't hold a candle to Kyle.

Mayzelle bustled in, widening her eyes when she saw Joy standing there, and enfolded her in a big hug. "We're so proud of you, Joyanne," she said. "Imagine a Yewville native becoming a big star! Why, next time you come home, I'll make sure we have a welcoming party. Like a parade with confetti and streamers on Palmetto Street? And you could ride on the back of the mayor's new convertible?"

Over Mayzelle's shoulder, Joy winked and grimaced in an expression that Dixie interpreted as "Help me!"

"We'd better hurry over to the Eat Right," Dixie said hastily, standing and shuffling her papers. "There's never a booth available once people start showing up for lunch."

Fluffy, bless her, chose that moment to heave herself to her feet and venture out from under Mayzelle's desk to beg for a treat, which afforded Dixie and Joy the perfect opportunity to escape. By the time they finished their lunch, which was interrupted by what seemed to be every friend and acquaintance that Joy ever knew before she left to pursue stardom, it was agreed that Joy would bring the salad for dinner and that Dixie would provide turkey breast and everything else. Dixie called Kyle on her cell phone to alert him, leaving a message on the home answering machine that he was sure to pick up when he got back from the hardware store where he'd gone to buy a better rake.

But when she reached home, lugging in the grocery bags by herself and wondering why Kyle wasn't there, she found a note he'd left on the kitchen table.

Dixie dear—gone for the afternoon, maybe the evening. Possibly longer. I'll call and explain later. Love, K

Love, K? What was that supposed to mean? Maybe it was nothing more than a convenient way to close the note. Or maybe…maybe? What if he was starting to feel the same way she was feeling about him?

She tried to call Kyle on his cell phone, but he didn't answer. That wasn't surprising. Still, she wondered why he hadn't previously mentioned his mysterious errand. Visions of him wrapped in Andrea's arms assailed her, imagination providing the details. Andrea would be overflowingly voluptuous, wear long dangling earrings and stiletto heels. She'd stuff herself into sexy see-through underwear and smell of musk. Her voice would be husky and deep.

When Kyle didn't call by the time she was supposed to put the turkey breast in the oven, Dixie contacted Joy, who was visiting at Bubba's house.

"Kyle's not here," Dixie said flatly even though it pained her to do so.

"You mean, he won't be back for dinner?" Dismay surfaced in Joy's tone and also a degree of mystification as if she couldn't imagine that Kyle could be absent after Dixie's glowing report.

"Uh, not sure," Dixie hedged, trying not to show her own disappointment. "His note wasn't all that specific."

"Well, at least he left a note." Joy muffled the receiver, then returned. "Dixie, Bubba says why don't we have dinner with Katie and him. Katie got the results of her sonogram, and their baby's a girl. They feel like celebrating with some of Bubba's home-brewed beer and barbecue."

"Okay," Dixie said with a sigh. If Kyle came back in time, he could follow later. "Can I bring something?"

"Katie says if you've got one of your fabulous desserts in the freezer, you might tote it along."

"I have half a caraway-seed cake that I was going to serve Memaw if she brought her friend Dottie over to see my new house this week. Don't worry, they'll be just as happy with brownies."

"Awesome! You'll have to give me your caraway-seed cake recipe before I leave. Bubba says to get here around six-thirty. Oh, I forgot, I have to drop off Mama's medicine at the house. How about if I stop by and bring you over here? I'm driving my Chevy, it'll be like old times."

"Okay, that sounds good."

"About six-fifteen?"

"Sure. Pick me up before you drop off the medicine so I can say hey to your mother. I haven't seen her in a couple of weeks."

"Right, will do. See you later, Dixie."

Slowly Dixie replaced the phone in its cradle then picked

it up again to dial Kyle's cell phone. All she got was a prere-corded message delivered by a female with a serious attitude problem. "Your call did not go through. Please try again later." She wondered what gave phone companies the right to unloose snotty disinterested voices on perfectly innocent people.

Sighing, she went to get the cake out of the freezer. Too bad Kyle wasn't around to eat it. He loved caraway-seed cake.

Before Joy arrived, Dixie dialed Kyle's cell number again. This time the call went through, but it rang and rang. Whatever Kyle was doing, she hoped he was enjoying it. She wouldn't be making another cake for a couple of weeks.

Plus, when she went to check on the new rake that Kyle had said he was going to buy, it wasn't there. The old one was in pieces on the workbench, the tines broken off.

What could have been so important that Kyle would go off before he brought the new rake home? Must have been something major.

Chapter Six

If someone ever ran a contest for the most irritating and annoying modern invention, the cell phone would win hands down. At least that's what Kyle fumed after he tried to call Dixie for the fourth time that afternoon and got the message "Service Unavailable."

He hadn't expected to be on his way to Camden so late in the day, but a call from Jarvis Wilfield had speared him into action. Kyle's main motivation for answering Wilfield's summons was that moving to South Carolina seemed like a better idea every day, and steady work hereabouts would make such a move even more likely.

When Jarvis called, he'd been in an agitated state of mind. "Mac McGehee was rushed to the hospital this morning," he told Kyle. "He's had a stroke, and with the Carolina Cup coming up at the end of the month besides." The Carolina Cup was one of two big steeplechase events of the year.

"What can I do to help?"

"Come over here and help me with Kingpin, one of our horses who is set to compete. He's thrown a shoe."

Kyle'd jotted down a few notes about the horse and the location of the stable. "I'll be there as soon as I can," he'd assured Wilfield, and now he was heading to Camden, singing along with WYEW and feeling good about his prospects.

If he'd been able to reach Dixie, perhaps she could have ridden along with him. He would have been grateful for the company. He recalled her mentioning that she had an appointment that afternoon, and there wasn't much he could do about that. He'd taken the time to leave Dixie a hastily written note, which he now realized he should have made more explicit. Perhaps he'd be able to reach her through his cell phone as soon as he came within range of a cell tower.

Kyle slowed his speed as he drove into the Camden city limits. He felt bad about not being able to explain to Dixie, but she'd understand. By this time, they were one hundred percent a couple.

And would be for quite some time if he had his way.

WHEN DIXIE AND JOY arrived at Bubba's house for dinner, Katie greeted them warmly at the door. She was a taffy-haired dynamo who was proud of her new belly bulge and immediately hustled Joy off to admire clothes for the coming baby. After spotting the sonogram of a fetus posted proudly on the refrigerator door, a precursor of all the snapshots and drawings to come, Dixie declined to "ooh" and "aah" over the layette for the time being. Despite her genuine happiness for Bubba and Katie, it rankled that she wasn't even a wife yet, much less an expectant mother.

Bubba and Katie's house was small and tidy, built forty years or so ago of redbrick made from native South Carolina clay. It was lovingly furnished with inviting furniture slipcovered in faded cotton prints—"shabby unchic" Katie called it.

Dixie always felt comfortable there due to the couple's match-less hospitality. However, on this visit, Bubba started teasing her big-time while the two of them were hanging out in the kitchen.

"You still keeping company with that Yankee?" Bubba asked, handing Dixie a cold beer. This was the polite Yewville way of asking if she and Kyle continued to live together.

"The Yankee's name is Kyle," Dixie informed him loftily. "Seems like you should remember it, since you were one of the first people I called to help him out. Not that you did," she added pointedly.

Bubba ignored the barb. "Well, *my* name is Charles," he said. "Right out of the chute everyone started calling me Bubba, and that's how I'm known to this day."

"It's understandable. Bubba means 'brother.' You were somebody's brother as soon as you were born, seeing as how your parents already had Fred."

"Why didn't they call Fred 'Bubba'?"

"Gosh, Charles, I have no idea. What does this have to do with Kyle?"

"Your boyfriend is referred to around town as 'the Yankee' on account of everyone has heard about what he was wearing when you found him. The poor guy might be stuck with that nickname for the rest of his life."

"I doubt that would bother him," Dixie said. She took a long swig of beer and changed the subject. "Awesome beer, Bubba."

"Milo says it's better than he can make."

"Oh, so you're hanging out with Milo?"

"We've been friends almost as long as you and I have," Bubba reminded her. He paused, shot her an inquisitive grin. "Why don't the two of you get back together?"

Dixie expelled a long sigh of impatience. "Hel-*lo?* Weren't we just talking about my new boyfriend, the Yankee?"

"Milo still likes you a lot. Dang, I never did understand why you two broke up."

"You wouldn't. Probably." Her feelings for Milo had been pure blah compared to what she had with Kyle.

"Try me. Talk to me. Why didn't you and Milo tie the knot?"

If Bubba was going to be difficult, she'd rock him. "Here's the truth of it, Bubba. I broke up with Milo because I didn't feel passion for him."

Bubba stared as if she had just stripped stark naked. *"Passion?"* he said in a shocked tone. They normally didn't discuss that sort of thing.

She narrowed her eyes, not ready to back off yet. "Like when you want to crawl right into a person, you're so attracted to him."

Bubba's face turned crimson and he appeared on the verge of swallowing his chin. "Uh, well, we shouldn't be talking about that."

"Then don't ever bring it up again."

"Not to worry. Geez, Dixie. I'm going to go get some of those boiled peanuts I stored in the garage." He slapped a baseball cap on backward and marched out.

Joy and Katie returned, both of them chattering about the baby's wardrobe. Joy reclaimed her bottle of beer. "I propose a toast to— What are you going to name her, Katie?"

"Marcella Jane Granthum," Katie announced. "Marcy for short."

"To Marcy," Joy said. The women clinked bottles except for Katie who had forsaken alcohol for the duration of her pregnancy.

Bubba came back. "I can't find the boiled peanuts that I had in the garage," he said to Katie.

"They're in the fridge, hon."

Bubba rummaged for the peanuts and emptied them into a dish. He put a paper bag on the floor for the shells. "Our Marcy's going to be the first of a bunch of born bricklayers named Granthum," he declared. He'd recently started a masonry business, which he ran with the help of his cousin, and had often bemoaned the fact that it was hard to find skilled masons these days.

"My little girl, a bricklayer?" Katie said in mock disbelief.

"I'll train her early, her and all the brothers and sisters she's going to have. That doesn't mean she can't wear a pretty pink dress with petticoats once in a while," Bubba said, all puffed up with fatherly pride.

Katie, Joy and Dixie started to laugh. "No one wears petticoats anymore," Joy said.

"I guess I have a few things to learn about raising little girls," Bubba said with a grin.

Past the gated bedroom door on the other side of the small dining room, Bubba's old coon dog, Minnie Pearl, wagged her tail, four puppies gamboling around and between her legs. Katie went to the kitchen sink where she began to mix dressing for slaw.

"I hope y'all are agreeable to barbecue," Katie said, glancing briefly over her shoulder. "How about you, Joyanne? Is pulled pork allowed on your diet?"

"I might have to make an exception so I can pig out on Bubba's 'cue," Joy said. "I'll compensate by not eating anything but lettuce and watercress tomorrow."

Bubba removed a couple of foam containers from the refrigerator. The containers held barbecue that he'd picked off the pig he'd roasted over his backyard pit last fall. "We'll heat the meat in the microwave and spread everything out on the counter so we can help ourselves," he said.

As Dixie and Joy pitched in, Katie glanced out the window where a red truck was pulling up beside the chinquapin tree. "You'd better get out another one of those barbecue containers, Bubba. Milo's here."

Dixie exchanged an alarmed glance with Joy. She certainly hadn't expected her old boyfriend to show up for dinner.

"I didn't invite him, but it's not unusual for Milo to stop in," Bubba said, observing Dixie's ill-concealed alarm.

Joy took the lead. "It'll be great to see him," she said. "We were both active in the theater group when we were kids."

"Milo checks on Minnie Pearl's pups a few times a week. Say's he's of a mind to buy one." Bubba tossed a peanut shell into the paper bag on the floor.

Katie smiled. "Oh, Bubba, you might as well give him his favorite, the little female. Then when she's grown, you two can go coon hunting together."

"Just like the old days when our daddies did the same thing," Bubba said. "Dad gum it, I believe I will give Milo that dog. I'll make enough money off the others to furnish the nursery any way you like." He and Katie shared a loving smile.

Dixie considered that she ought to be going but didn't have her car. Milo came in, all smiles at seeing Joy, or were the smiles for Dixie? He enveloped Joy in a big hug, proclaimed that her bouncy new hairstyle was awesome and that she was prettier than ever. This might be a good time to go powder her nose, but before Dixie could make a hasty exit,

Milo hugged her, as well. She escaped as soon as possible, insisting on setting the table so Katie could sit down and prop her swollen feet on a chair seat for a few minutes.

Milo's curly hair looked as if he'd tried to smooth it down with some kind of gunk. Everything about him was too tidy— unwrinkled white shirt tucked neatly into khaki pants, shiny loafers without a smudge of dirt, fingernails trimmed just so. Of course, eating had to wait while Milo brought himself up to speed on Bubba's beer.

This led to reminiscing among the five of them. Dixie, keeping her distance from Milo by perching on a stool at the breakfast bar, attempted to return the topic to the here and now, but the conversation worked its way back to the chilly fall night when they'd all gone cow tipping in Mr. Hibble's field.

After they laughed over that, Milo recalled the year that Bubba treated himself to an orange-and-purple Mohawk hair- cut and was thus single-handedly responsible for the institu- tion of a dress code at Yewville High. More seriously, Katie, who was a year younger than they were, mentioned the day their assistant principal, Mr. Dacoti, was wounded in the eye by a student who attacked him with a numchuk, a martial arts weapon that shouldn't have been on campus in the first place.

It had been years before the shootings at Columbine, but in the space of a few short minutes after Mr. Dacoti was car- ried away in an ambulance, an atmosphere of fear settled over the high-school campus.

Dixie hadn't recalled that day in years. She'd been a fif- teen-year-old sophomore and worried that more violence was imminent. Rumblings of student discontent had been reported earlier in the day, so anything could happen. When Milo discovered Dixie cowering behind her locker door, he had immediately shepherded her off campus and driven her home. Her mother, already alerted to trouble at the school by the Yewville grapevine, had thanked him profusely.

Fortunately, the campus remained peaceful. Both Dixie and Milo were penalized for skipping classes, but she'd never blamed him for taking charge that day. It was the first time Dixie had known that Milo really cared for her.

Remembering that day made her smile at him, and his eyes lit up. *Damn,* Dixie thought. *This beer must be much higher in alcohol content than the store-bought kind.* She had unwittingly lowered the barriers that she'd thrown up between them earlier. As the others started to talk about what had happened to the rest of their high-school group in the years since graduation, she excused herself and went to play with the puppies on the other side of the gate barrier.

A tactical mistake. Milo soon joined her, smiling goofily. She recognized that grin, all right. She'd spotted it on his face at church the Sunday he proposed to her.

"I'm going to take that pup over there," he said, gesturing toward the brown-spotted one that was poking at a red rubber bone with its nose.

"What will you name her?" Anything to keep him on the safe subject of the dog.

"Starbright." Milo glanced at her sideways out of the corner of his eye.

Oh, drat. The name struck a too-familiar chord. On their first date, a church hayride, as they jounced over a rutted country road surrounded by energetically necking couples, the stars above had started to pop out spectacularly and Milo had recited a poem.

Star light, star bright,
First star I see tonight
I wish I may, I wish I might
Have the wish I wish tonight.

It was many months before Milo admitted that his wish had been that Dixie would kiss him good-night. Well, she had, and they'd started going steady two weeks later. It had been a good decision at the time, she now realized. All through high school they'd been companions, friends, and finally, shortly before they broke up, lovers. But she'd passed on marrying Milo. And that had been the right decision, too.

"Starbright is a nice name," she murmured, not giving anything away.

"I'm glad you like it," Milo said, seeking something in her expression that he clearly didn't find. Dixie recognized the disappointment that shadowed his eyes ever so briefly before she turned away.

"Come on, you two," Katie called from the kitchen. "Barbecue's on."

Dixie gratefully returned to the kitchen, where Milo kept sending beseeching glances across the small kitchen table as they ate. Fortunately, it wasn't necessary to talk much. Joy recited interesting anecdotes about her new life, and Bubba was expansive about his impending fatherhood. Apparently no one noticed that Dixie was uncharacteristically quiet.

The truth was that her mind had wandered back to Kyle. Before she left home she'd written a note of her own, using the saltshaker to pin hers down alongside his on the kitchen table. She'd written down Bubba's address and phone number and asked Kyle to call her either at that number or on her cell when he got home. But as dinner wore on, as they cleaned up the kitchen, still no Kyle.

By the time Katie suggested that they adjourn to the living room for cake and coffee, Dixie was glancing at her watch for maybe the tenth time since they sat down to dinner. Bubba and Milo chatted about the best treatment for nematodes in soybeans, a topic of some interest in this rural area. Dixie filled Joy and Katie in on her new career and asked their opinion about accepting the cat Leland had offered. When Bubba brought out the Rummikub game, it was Joy who pleaded early exhaustion so she and Dixie could leave.

"Jet lag," Joy said. "Flying cross-country cuts me down worse than anything." She claimed to have done her share of traveling from coast to coast lately, seeing as her agent's main office was in New York.

When Joy made it clear that she and Dixie needed to leave, Milo said he had to get up early the next morning. They all trooped to the door and hugged Katie and Bubba, thanking them for the delicious meal.

"Wait a minute, Dixie," Bubba said. He disappeared into the kitchen and returned with a bottle of home brew. "Might as well give the Yankee a taste of really good beer."

Dixie tucked the bottle under her arm. "Thanks, Bubba. Kyle may call you for the recipe."

Bubba winked. "Anytime."

Milo gazed wistfully at Dixie for a long moment, and he kept trying to catch her eye on the way out to the street where they all were parked. Dixie pretended she didn't notice; she was uncomfortable with Milo's overt longing and wasted no time sliding into Joy's old Chevy.

"Fast enough exit?" Joy asked with a sly grin.

"What do you mean?"

"I saw how you were avoiding Milo's glances, his effort to sit next to you in the living room, all that stuff."

"You read me right, girlfriend."

"Let's get out of here. I'm sure you have other plans for the evening."

Dixie smiled, though with marked restraint. "I hope so," she said.

When Joy turned the key in the car's ignition, all they heard was a disheartening click. "Uh-oh," Joy said. "This sounds serious." She tried the key again and this time elicited a tired groan from the battery, which engendered an even more tired groan from Joy.

"I should have asked Daddy to charge the battery, but Mama claimed she'd started this car up only a couple of weeks ago," Joy said. "I'm planning to sell it. I figured that I'd at least be able to use it while I'm here."

"Maybe you should try to start it again," Dixie suggested. The Chevy had been in great mechanical shape when Joy left for California.

"Joyanne? Dixie?" Milo had rolled down the window of his pickup. "Got a problem?"

Dixie stared steadfastly ahead as Joy got out of the car and slammed the door. "Dead battery. Can't get it going." Crickets shrilled in the shrubbery, and somewhere a cat yowled.

"We could call Hub," Dixie called out the window, naming the mechanic who had bought Carrie's garage. "He could be here in a few minutes."

"No need," Milo said. "I can drive both of you home. You're hardly out of my way."

"Come on, Dixie," Joy said. "We might as well. I really am too tired to deal with this right now."

Hearing their voices, Katie and Bubba switched the porch light back on and opened the screen door.

"What's wrong?" they chorused.

"Dead battery," Joy called back.

"I've got jumper cables in my car. Won't take me but a moment," Bubba offered.

"I'll call you tomorrow, maybe we can do it then. Thanks anyway." Joy grabbed her purse, and Dixie climbed out of the Chevy. She'd rather not ride home with Milo, but what choice did she have? The last thing she'd do was cause a scene over this.

Milo reached across the front seat and threw open the passenger door of his truck. "I'll drop Joyanne off first," he said, which was logical because her parents' house was only a mile or so away.

This meant that Dixie would have to sit in the middle of the pickup's bench seat next to Milo, so she suppressed a sigh and got in. Joy climbed in after her. The whole way to Joy's parents' house, Dixie kept her eyes focused on the fuzzy black-and-white dice swinging from the rearview mirror. They made her dizzy, twirling around like that.

Joy was yawning by the time they dropped her off at the asbestos-shingled house where she'd grown up. Through the picture window, they could see her mother dipping up popcorn as she watched TV. "Thanks for the lift, Milo," Joy said. "Dixie, I'll call you in the morning."

As soon as Joy was out of the vehicle, Dixie slid away from Milo and toward the door. He waited until Joy went inside, then backed out of the driveway. The silence was uneasy between them, and Dixie turned her head away to gaze out the window at the fields slipping by, most of them already plowed for planting soybeans or cotton or tobacco. The moon was full and the sky full of stars, bringing to mind that silly poem again. *Star light, star bright, first star I see tonight, I wish I may, I wish I might...*

Tonight she'd wish that Kyle would be at home waiting for her when she got there. No question about that.

While Milo attempted to draw her out, Dixie replied to his remarks with as few words as possible, unerringly polite but not enthusiastic. Milo began telling her about buying acreage for his nursery business, a story which wasn't of much interest to her.

After several minutes of Milo's throwing out conversation starters, he must have grown weary of her monosyllabic replies because he lapsed into quiet long before he turned down her driveway. As they passed the sasanqua hedge, Dixie caught herself leaning forward in the seat in hopes of spotting a telltale gleam of chrome from Kyle's truck, but it wasn't parked in its usual space.

Over and above the letdown, she entertained the scary notion that Kyle might have skipped town. Gone back to Andrea. Left without telling her. But no, he'd left a note earlier. A kind of sweet note, actually, and he'd signed it *Love, K.*

"Thanks for the ride, Milo," Dixie said as she swung down out of the truck. Belatedly, as he slid out from under the steering wheel, she realized that Milo was going to walk her to the door. She almost objected before deciding that an argument would be more trouble than it was worth. Dixie's house was dark, unoccupied, and any true gentlemen would insist on seeing a woman safely inside.

She'd forgotten to leave the porch light on, and because she was still carrying the clammy bottle of beer, she fumbled with her key. Without a word, Milo took it from her and inserted it in the lock. He opened the door, and the glow of the night-light illuminated his face as she turned toward him to thank him again for the ride.

Perhaps she was sending mixed signals after all. Milo's expression was one of hopefulness, of affection.

"It was wonderful seeing you, Dixie," he said, a hitch in his voice.

Not, she thought as she stepped backward to minimize what she was pretty sure Milo had in mind. Too late. He firmly placed his hands on her shoulders and wasted no time in lowering his mouth to hers. She clamped her teeth shut and held her breath, leaning out of it. No matter how far backward she bent, Milo stuck like glue. Milo was still kissing her enthusiastically when bright headlights sliced across the hedge and Kyle's truck pulled into the driveway.

The beer bottle fell on the steps and broke in an explosion of foam and glass.

FIFTEEN MINUTES LATER, Dixie was repentant and regretful, not that it seemed to help.

"All I did was talk to Andrea on the phone," Kyle said angrily. "*You* were *kissing* Milo." It was the first time he had ever raised his voice to her, and that alone made her forget how sorry she was.

"Milo was kissing *me*," she informed him. "For which I should have slapped him, maybe." They had adjourned to her bedroom after Milo left, and Kyle paced to the far end of it. She pulled off her shoes, wet with beer. "Or hit him over the head with the beer bottle," she added on second thought. She sniffed at her hands; they smelled beery, too. Beer tasted better than it smelled, that was for sure.

"Why didn't you?"

"Because you were charging up the slope to the house and I figured if there was any physical punishment to be inflicted, you'd be the one to administer it."

"I wanted to deck him, but he got away too fast."

"Fortunately. The police chief and Milo are second cousins."

"Everybody's related around here," Kyle said, sounding none too happy about it.

She said, "One of the reasons I hoped you'd come over to Bubba and Katie's tonight was that it's time for you to meet my friends."

Kyle sighed. "I had business. Turns out the farrier in Camden is going to be out of commission for a while, and there's work for me there." Quickly he outlined the opportunities available to him.

"Now I understand better than I did," she allowed in a more subdued tone. "If we'd talked earlier, I never would have become so upset."

"I couldn't reach you. Look, your friend Joy sounds like a charming person. I would have liked to spend the evening with all of you. I couldn't this time."

At least he'd said *this time*. That implied that there'd be another one.

"What was with the beer, anyway?" he asked.

"Bubba's into brewing it these days. He sent you a bottle." She'd hated dropping the beer on Milo's foot, but when Kyle drove up, she'd suddenly remembered how the bird flapping out of nowhere had put the kibosh on her first necking session with him and figured she needed an interrupting factor of a similar sort in order to confuse things.

"And you broke it? That's a shame."

"Maybe you could lick the beer off my feet," she said grimly. "That's where most of it is."

He stared for a moment and apparently decided she was joking. "Too kinky for my present mood," he said.

She knew things would be all right then, or at least sort of all right. She closed her eyes for a long moment, opened them. "Kyle, the whole incident is over and done with. Let's let it go." Having had enough arguing, she went into the bathroom and started to remove her clothes.

"Of course, there is still the little matter of your kissing Milo," Kyle pointed out from where he stood. "And him slinking away, guilty as hell."

She turned toward him, half undressed. She ran water into the sink and tossed her reeking slacks into it. "All right. I'm denying that I returned his kiss, but suppose I did? What would it mean? Nothing major, merely good night. I wasn't about to invite him in. What would we do? Sleep together while I wait for you to show up? With your clothes in my closet and your toothbrush in the toothbrush holder?"

"The toothbrush holder has more than one slot."

"Kyle, I'm a one-man woman. Always have been, always will be. Right now you're the man in my life. I don't want anyone else."

This speech completed, she took her time turning on the water for the shower. He was still watching when she stepped under the spray. For a moment, she thought that he might join her, but when she emerged from the bathroom, Kyle was already under the bedcovers, his back to her.

She waited a moment for him to speak or move. He didn't, so she slid under the blankets and switched out the light.

As her eyes adjusted to the darkness, she waited for Kyle to say something, anything. Surely he'd speak or, well, do something else. For instance, usually at night he reached for her and pulled her close. They'd recount the day's activities and share a laugh or two before falling asleep. Tonight was different.

His back was only inches away, but it might have been a wall of impenetrable steel rather than mere flesh and blood. She shifted onto her side facing him and listened to his breathing, which was steady and shallow, not deep or regular enough for sleep. So he was as awake as she was, and he probably didn't know what to do to put an end to this impasse any more than she did.

Scenes flitted through her mind as she tried to figure out what to do. Milo's laughable expression of surprise when Kyle drove up in her driveway. Bubba and Katie holding hands when they sat side by side on the couch. Her sister's confidences about how happy she was with her new husband when Dixie had gone to visit them in Europe. And further back in time, Voncille's determination to make a go of her marriage. Voncille had been only seventeen years old when she and Skeeter eloped and were married in a ninety-nine-dollar wedding at South of the Border, the local favorite for quickie weddings, but something her cousin had said back then stuck in Dixie's mind.

"Skeeter and I make it a point never to go to bed angry. We always reconcile before we go to sleep. Memaw's the one who gave us that good advice. She said that if you make up right away, you don't give an argument a chance to grow into a major snit."

Thinking about this, Dixie decided it would serve no good purpose to remain angry with Kyle. She believed he could have been more considerate about informing her where he was and what he was doing. Now, at least, she understood why it was important to him to go to Camden. In his way, he was taking steps to make it possible for them to stay together.

She extended a tentative hand toward Kyle, drew it back. Then she reached out again. This time she touched warm skin, and his muscles tensed almost imperceptibly beneath her fingertips. She was overcome by a rush of tenderness.

"Kyle," she whispered into the dark between them. "Don't do this."

A long moment passed during which Dixie wasn't sure if Kyle would accept her attempt at making peace. Then he sighed and rolled toward her, depressing the mattress so that she tilted in his direction. Her feet slipped between his, as they had on so many happier nights, and his eyes were luminous in the light from the window.

"I hate it when we fight," he said. His hand stole up to trace the outline of her chin, to cup her cheek.

"Me, too," she said, tears filling her eyes and blurring his face. One tear trickled down her cheek and onto Kyle's hand.

"Oh, Dixie," he said. "Come here."

He wrapped her in his arms, and she pressed her damp cheek against his chest. The long naked length of him eased against her, but Dixie had no desire to get sexual. What she needed desperately was reassurance that their relationship was too important to allow silly misunderstandings to drive them apart.

"I'm sorry," Dixie said. "I should have stopped Milo before he kissed me. I could have, I guess." The admission was difficult to make, but she was being truthful. Subconsciously she may have wanted proof that Milo cared about her when she wasn't so sure that Kyle did.

"Who could pass up a chance to kiss you?" Kyle said with unexpected humor. "I'm thinking of doing it myself."

She raised her lips to his and they kissed, her arms finding their way up around his neck. If only he would say he loved her! She longed to tell him how much she loved him, but instead of talking after ending the kiss, they lay quietly, heartbeats and breaths settling into the same rhythm.

"I don't suppose you'd like to go steady, would you?" Kyle said after a while.

"Ask me."

"Would you like to go steady, Dixie?"

"Maybe. Yes, I would."

"Great. It's settled. No more smooching other guys." He kissed her slowly and lingeringly, sighing as she settled closer to him. A few seconds later, Kyle was asleep. Dixie lay awake for a long time, listening to him breathe and staring into the darkness.

Chapter Seven

The day after their big blowup over Milo, and as relieved as he was that it hadn't escalated out of control, Kyle realized that his rapprochement with Dixie was fragile. Even though they made love first thing in the morning, slowly and tenderly refilling each other from a bottomless well of sexual pleasure, their talk afterward was strained. At breakfast he was sure he'd go bonkers if she mentioned the Maine coon cat man one more time.

Dixie seemed totally unaware of his annoyance. "Leland Porter—that's the cat man—he's going back to Maryland soon, and he's lost patience with whether I'm going to accept that cat or not. Then Mayzelle mentioned last thing yesterday that Leland is going to drop off some papers at the office and I should be there when he does, which will be early this morning, she says."

Kyle wondered how she could talk of something so trivial. Uppermost in his mind was the new commitment of exclusivity that he and Dixie had made to each other last night. This was the first step toward something more meaningful. For him it was a major milestone, and he took it seriously. And the commitment wasn't all of it. He was falling in love with Dixie. However, expressing his emotions had never been easy for him, and he wasn't sure he wanted to open up to her. At least not yet.

But there was something he could do to let her know he cared about her. That he cared *for* her.

"Dixie," he said into the silence. "I'm going to pay my share around this house. I shouldn't be living here and letting you shoulder all the expenses."

Her expression softened as her gaze met his. "Kyle, that's sweet of you." She sounded surprised.

"I mean it."

She frowned slightly. "You wouldn't have to. I mean, buying food once in a while is nice, and contributing a bottle of wine now and then, and—"

"We should make out a budget. How about if we talk about it later?" *I wouldn't offer if I didn't love you,* he thought. *Want to love you? Almost love you?*

Coming from the emotional wasteland of his childhood, which featured an absent mother and an unemotional father, he didn't know how to frame the words. Didn't feel right saying them.

She stood up and walked over to him, sliding her hands up around his neck. "Thanks. Your offer means a lot to me."

He kissed her before she pulled away. While she went to check her answering machine for messages, Kyle poured himself a second cup of coffee. "You might tell me where I should plant the dogwoods," he said when she returned to the kitchen. "I dug them up special from the woods day before yesterday." He intended to plant the trees before returning to Camden today.

"Oh, anywhere," Dixie said with a dismissive flap of her hand.

"Do you know if what I heard from a guy at the Eat Right yesterday was true—that when you transplant dogwood trees dug up in the woods, you have to position them as they were?"

"I've never heard of that," Dixie said, clearly distracted.

"It would require that the side of the trunk that faced the north in the woods again face the north when placed in the new hole."

"I could ask Memaw and give you a call."

"The guy that suggested it said it's not a good idea to confuse the plant." He didn't add that, since he was considering transplanting himself, the dogwood could be a test case.

"I'll try to find out. Right now I've got to run." Dixie leaned across the table for a quick goodbye kiss and grabbed her briefcase. "See you later. What are your plans today?"

"I have things to do in Camden." He'd promised to trim the hooves of a Tennessee walker, then he'd check on Mac McGehee's prognosis.

She looked surprised, though not enough to ask questions. Or maybe she was just in a rush. "Okay. You can tell me all about it over dinner. How about one of those roasted chickens that the deli does so well? I'll make yellow rice to go with it."

"It's a plan."

Kyle rinsed his cup off in the sink as he watched Dixie rushing along the path to the garage. His mind was full of new resolutions. He no longer wanted to be poised on the cusp between past and present. He was charging headlong into the future. Today he would phone Andrea and tell her to stop calling him. He'd inform her that it was over, finally over, and

she'd better move on with her life. Then he and Dixie would
be free to—well, whatever. And he would learn to say—well,
whatever—if only he could work around to it.

After he'd planted the dogwoods—north to north, south to
south—Kyle headed for the office in the house, where he
dialed Andrea's phone number at work. She'd be harried at
this time of year due to its being tax season, which could work
to his advantage because she probably wouldn't be able to talk
long. He was surprised when she answered the phone herself.

"Ludovici Tax Service."

"Andrea," he said.

"Kyle?" she replied cautiously.

"Right."

She breathed out an impatient sigh, a sure sign of stress.
"At least you're not that nasty client who keeps calling and
whining about the intricacies of IRS Form 4797. Wait a minute." She shuffled papers, scraped chair legs across the floor.
Kyle pictured Andrea moving swiftly into her private office
and settling down on the big wing chair usually reserved for
clients. He almost wished he had called to complain about
IRS Form 4797, whatever that was. It might be a whole lot
easier than what he had in mind.

"All right, I can talk," Andrea said. "Where are you, anyway?"

"I'm still in South Carolina."

"When will you be home?"

He cleared his throat. "The truth is, I might stay here."

"Why?" Her tone was strident, and he held the phone away
from his ear.

"Reasons. Look, Andrea, it's over between us."

A long silence, then an incredulous laugh. "I hoped—

Well, as you're aware, I have community-theater tickets, and the last play of the season is in a few weeks."

He wasted no time setting her straight. "Andrea, you broke up with me, remember?"

"I shouldn't have done it, I realize that now. I miss you, Kyle."

"Andrea—"

"You've met someone, haven't you?" she interrupted. "It's a woman, right?"

"What, you think it could be a guy?"

"Of course not," Andrea said, her voice spiking with impatience.

"Yes, I've met someone, but there are good business opportunities here, as well."

"Like what?"

She was no doubt hoping that he'd found another way to make a living besides shoeing horses, and he might as well disabuse her of that notion immediately. "I shoe horses for a living, Andrea. That's what I do."

"So in South Carolina they have more horses than we do in Ohio? Or more horseshoes? Or what?" Definite sarcasm here.

He sighed. "Take my word for it, there's plenty of work. The cost of living is lower, winters are milder and you know how I hate shoveling snow."

Right now he could imagine her knotting her brows together as she often did when crossed, but he didn't anticipate the explosive nature of her next comments. "Kyle, that is the stupidest thing I ever heard in my life. What could possibly inspire you to live among a bunch of rednecks? When you have a nice apartment here, besides. And your fellow reenactors, don't forget them. Elliott asked me again if you're going to come to the reenactment in Virginia. You need to call him, Kyle, and let him know. Hush, Twinkle, no more treats for you till after you poo-poo. Stop, Twinks. *Stop.*"

Kyle suppressed a smile at this byplay with the dog. He'd all but forgotten how Andrea would inject comments to Twinkle in the middle of the most meaningful discussions.

"Kyle? Are you there, Kyle?"

"I'm here," he said with considerable forbearance.

"Good. I intend to talk some sense into you."

"Andrea, don't call me anymore. If you do, I won't answer my phone, and—"

"Like you've been answering it anyway," she scoffed. "Honestly, Kyle, you make everything so difficult."

He made things difficult? When Andrea never passed up an opportunity to inform him of her contempt for his work and refused to consider that this time he meant what he said?

"Goodbye, Andrea," he said, hoping it was for the last time in his life. Getting away from her for a period of time had allowed him the space and time to reassess his life's purpose, and shoring up other people wasn't it.

"Kyle!" she yelped as he clicked off the phone. Despite his relief at putting an unpleasant conversation behind him, Kyle didn't feel good about hurting someone's feelings, though he reminded himself that Andrea never minded hurting his.

The ordeal of the past few minutes put him in need of time for reflection, so he decided that today he'd take the back road to Camden as Kathy Lou had suggested the last time he stopped in the Eat Right.

He checked his supplies and started out. He'd anticipated mulling over his words with Andrea; instead he kept recalling that rush of anger, the churning of his stomach yesterday evening when he realized that another man's lips were affixed to Dixie's. He'd fantasized about jumping back in his truck and driving away, as if in fleeing he could obliterate the scene from his consciousness. He'd stayed and played the scene out to its desired end, which was being in Dixie's bed with her, holding her close, making sure that the other man in her life didn't wedge himself between them, either literally or figuratively.

After a while, he became absorbed in exploring side roads, one of which led to an old gristmill, another that took him past a creek blocked by a large beaver dam. He stopped at a roadside grocery store and bought lunch, which he ate near the edge of a small lake. This was beautiful country. He could do a lot worse than to live here.

And the bonus to the move was that he'd be near Dixie Lee Smith.

DIXIE TOOK WEDNESDAY afternoon off from work to help Memaw Frances with her spring cleaning. Memaw's arthritis prevented her from such chores as scrubbing the woodwork in her house, and Dixie and Carrie had always pitched in with the heavy work. Now that Carrie was gone, Voncille took her place. At first Dixie's cousin wasn't much help, considering that she brought along Petey, her youngest. He was a cherubic three-year-old, but he required an awful lot of attention. Finally Voncille put him down for a nap on Memaw's big brass bed.

Voncille switched the radio to WYEW Yew-and-Me Country, grabbed a sponge mop and adjourned to the kitchen, where she vigorously started to swab the floor, her thick red braid swinging across her back. Dixie stood on a ladder cleaning the crystal chandelier in the dining room, and Memaw was comfortably ensconced at the hall table polishing the good sterling to the beat of a Garth Brooks song. Silver to the right of her, silver to the left of her; all of it dark with tarnish. Memaw had been putting off this chore for over a year.

"Dixie, how're you and Kyle doing?" Voncille wanted to know, swinging the mop in time to the music. She wore her usual baggy denim overalls and a white T-shirt, apparel that seldom varied from day to day.

"Fine." Dixie concentrated on wiping vinegar water on the crystal pendants. According to the household-hints column she read every week in the *Yewville Messenger,* it would sparkle them up considerably.

"He has a solid, square jaw, too. That bespeaks determination," Memaw opined. She gave a tray an extra flourish and set it aside, all shiny and ready for Sunday's family dinner.

"Cro-Magnon man had a square jaw. What good did it do? He's extinct." This from Voncille.

"Kyle is very handsome," Dixie said. "I like the looks of him."

Voncille didn't glance up from her mopping as she spoke. "I liked the looks of Skeeter, too. I spotted him at the tractor pull and fell instantly in love. I mean, it was a whole new thing—colors were brighter, music was prettier, and when he winked at me, life was so completely perfect that I realized I had to be with him forever." As she leaned on the mop for a moment, an expression of fond remembrance passed across her features.

Dixie stopped what she was doing. "Was it really like that, Vonnie? Right away?"

"Uh-huh. Like lightning hit us and knocked us for a loop."

"Amazing," Dixie replied, trying to recall if that's the way it was when she first met Kyle. No, mostly she'd been worried about him wobbling around the parking lot on legs that could hardly hold him up. He'd been awfully disoriented. She wouldn't compare the experience to being struck by lightning. It was more like stumbling upon a piece of jewelry in the dirt and not knowing if it was real gold until you'd washed it off.

"Has Kyle been wearing his blue uniform lately?" Memaw asked. "Doc Johnson's assistant said he had it on when he came in to get his tooth fixed."

"That's his reenacting uniform," Dixie said. "He only wears it when there's a battle."

Memaw looked down her nose at that. "Kyle ought to have something better to do with his time than wearing a Yankee uniform. My ancestors are spinning in their graves to think you're dating a Bluecoat."

"These ancestors in their graves, I seriously doubt that they're thinking anything," Dixie said dryly.

"He's not only a Bluecoat, but one named Sherman," Voncille added, returning to her mopping.

Dixie had never mentioned Kyle's last name around her family. She gestured wildly at Voncille, making a zipping motion across her mouth that her cousin was slow to comprehend. Behind Memaw's back, Voncille held her hands out in a palms-up, as if to say, *"Huh?"*

"Excuse me? I must be getting as deaf as Claudia because I didn't hear a thing you said." Memaw shot Voncille a look, which could have meant she'd heard but needed time to come up with a reply. On the other hand, it could also have meant she *hadn't* heard. You could never tell with Memaw.

"Vonnie, bring me a better rag, will you, please? This one's too linty."

Voncille reached for an old cloth diaper, handed it to Memaw.

Memaw tossed the other rag aside. "Dixie, it so happens I've heard from Kathy Lou that Kyle caught you kissing Milo at the back door one night," Memaw said. "She told me about it the other day."

Voncille dropped the mop. Her eyebrows flew clear up into her bangs. "Is that true?"

Voncille knew very well that Kathy Lou never lied.

"Yes, but it wasn't anything. Just a peck." Dixie went on wiping crystals.

Memaw frowned at that. "You're being awfully close-mouthed about it, Dixie. If a woman doesn't run on about the man in her life, something is wrong between them. Stop trying to hide it and fess up."

"Nothing's wrong, exactly," Dixie said, realizing there was no way out of this discussion.

"So what's going on?" Voncille asked. She had completely given up trying to mop by this time.

Dixie figured she might as well spill the beans. "He's—he's—well, Kyle's a real Yankee. His forebears did happen to be real important to the Union cause."

"Oh, well. That war was so long ago as to be insignificant," Voncille opined.

"What's over is over," Dixie agreed. "The point is, one of Kyle's *ancestors* was by no means insignificant. Not that this is a problem for me. The Great Unpleasantness was a long time ago."

Memaw regarded Dixie with something less than understanding. "That's easy for you to say. When I was growing up back in the 1920s, my grandfather and great-uncles were still around to tell us how Sherman's troops rode through

Yewville and camped by the Allentown Church. My great-uncle Addison's farm was ransacked by foragers who emptied every feather tick into the yard and rode off with his family's squealing pigs under their arms. His wife buried their silver in the swamp and never was able to tell anyone where to find it before she died in childbirth later that year. Not—" Memaw cast a rueful glance at all the silver still left to polish "—that I care if it's ever found."

Dixie drew a deep bolstering breath. "Everyone knows the war meant hard times for folks around here. But those people are gone. If someone's relatives were involved in the Civil War, so what? And if Kyle's hobby involves making people understand that both sides suffered, that everyone who fought and died should be memorialized, I'd say that's a good thing."

"My great-uncle would have tanned my hide if I'd said any such thing. Plus, the South Carolina State House still has Yankee bullet holes that were left unrepaired so no one would ever forget that we were defeated, occupied and stripped of our wealth, our culture and our heritage. To add insult to injury, the rest of the country is always putting us down and calling us dumb, redneck and racist, like we're not supposed to have enough sense to mind it." Memaw's mouth clamped into an uncompromising line.

Dixie climbed down from the ladder and sat on a chair beside Memaw. "You and I don't know one single person who is dumb, redneck or racist, and it's as unfair of us to judge Kyle as it is when we're judged by those who don't know us." She paused and took the plunge. "Memaw, Kyle's great-great-great-grandfather was a famous Union general. Kyle's full name is Kyle Tecumseh Sherman, Memaw." Dixie kept her gaze steady while her grandmother absorbed this information.

"As in William Tecumseh Sherman." Memaw's expression had taken on a steeliness, familiar only because it was the same way she communicated displeasure when one of the family shared the information that they didn't intend to be at church on Sunday.

"I've been reluctant to tell you. I grew up knowing how people feel about General Sherman around here."

"The general must have been a despicable man," Memaw said darkly, not bothering to hide her disdain.

"Who knows? Maybe in private life he had grandkids that he liked to bounce on his knee. Maybe he told funny jokes and—"

"His expression was what I'd call forbidding. Just check his picture in the encyclopedia," Memaw said, her tone brooking no objection. She seemed to draw herself together. "Well. I won't tell anyone at the United Daughters of the Confederacy meeting next week who Kyle is. They'd likely make me clean up the kitchen after our meetings for, oh, the next ten years. Harboring a Yankee! Feeding him my fried chicken! I can't believe I've done that." But a smile twitched at the corners of Memaw's mouth.

"Kyle and his reenactor friends and the United Daughters of the Confederacy have the same aim, preserving history, so that's something you all have in common."

"I suppose that's true," Memaw said reluctantly.

"You like Kyle," Dixie reminded her. "He's making you a special birdhouse for out on the porch."

"Well, you tell Kyle it better not be for housing Yankee birds, like those nasty starlings that come through and make so much noise on their winter migration. I'll have my birdhouse inhabited by nice Southern birds—mockingbirds, maybe."

Dixie smiled at Memaw in relief. The worst was over, and she regretted that she hadn't been more upfront about Kyle's ancestry from the beginning. "I'll make you a special little real estate sign to hang on that birdhouse," she promised. "One that says, For Rent, Mockingbirds Only."

"You might get in trouble with some government housing authority over that one. You're not supposed to discriminate. Didn't they teach you that in real estate school?" Voncille asked.

"It's okay if it's only birds," Dixie said jokingly.

"Vonnie, will you get me some of that iced tea out of the refrigerator? We all need a work break," observed Memaw.

"I brought cookies, too." Voncille went to get them, and Dixie gave Memaw a quick hug.

"Kyle really thinks you're special," she told her grandmother.

"As he should."

"Right." Dixie beamed at her.

"Well, Kyle may be a Yankee, but at least he doesn't have a pointy head. That's real important, Dixie Lee. Real important."

"I'd say there's more relevant things. Like whether he's good in the sack," Voncille said as she handed them each a tall glass of iced tea.

"Vonnie!" Memaw said, scandalized.

"I'm not telling. Memaw might see fit to repeat it at the UDC meeting," Dixie retorted self-righteously.

"Not that anyone there would be interested," Memaw said with a certain feigned hauteur.

"Of course not," chorused Dixie and Voncille, each of them poking the other in the ribs.

"Mom-*my!*" Petey's voice came wailing down the hall.

"Short nap," Voncille remarked. "Remind me not to feed that kid M&Ms after lunch anymore."

"Seems like maybe they did find that silver in the swamp," Memaw mused as she resumed shining a big teapot. "Otherwise why would I have so much of it to take care of?"

Well, that went pretty well, Dixie congratulated herself. If Memaw could accept Kyle for the fine person he was, anyone could.

Next she'd work on Bubba.

AS IT TURNED OUT, Dixie didn't have long to wait until Bubba dropped by to assess matters for himself.

"Dixie!" Bubba leaned out the window of his pickup truck. It was late afternoon, and she was walking back to the house after checking the mailbox.

She stopped leafing through envelopes and waved. "What's new, Bubba?" He had another man in the truck with him, and his old coon dog, Minnie Pearl, was riding in the bed of the pickup, her tail wagging faster than Odella Hatcher's tongue, and that was saying something.

"I'm on my way back from Bishopville. You busy?"

"Just ironing. Kyle's in the garage, building birdhouses."

"I heard about your Yankee's hobby from Mayzelle. Say, would Katie like one of them birdhouses?"

"I'm sure she would. Why don't you come in and check them out."

"Will do," he said. He steered the truck into the driveway and parked it beside Kyle's. By the time he and his passenger got out, Dixie had walked around the house.

"Dixie, remember my cousin Chad. You've met at some time or another."

"Why, sure we have. Hi, Chad, how have you been?" She recalled double-dating with him back when he'd been a star football player at Robert E. Lee Academy in Bishopville.

"Good to see you again, Dixie," Chad said.

"Kyle?" she called into the garage. "Bubba's here, and he's brought his cousin."

Kyle walked out. He was wiping his hands with a rag. "Paint thinner," he explained apologetically as Bubba offered his hand.

"It don't matter," Bubba said. "I've thinned paint a few times myself."

After they all shook hands, Bubba held out a bottle of beer. "I heard you didn't get a chance to sample any of this," he said to Kyle. "Milo told me that Dixie dropped the bottle before she got it in the house."

That's all Dixie needed, a reminder of that night. "Let's don't go there," she said hastily.

"You guys can come in and keep me company while I paint," Kyle said.

"If you don't mind, I'll get Chad and me a beer from the cooler in my truck first." Bubba took off.

Dixie said, "I'm going to finish ironing."

"Sure, go ahead," Kyle said, smiling at her. "The guys and I can visit."

She started toward the house. She hadn't realized it before, but likely, Kyle was lonely for male companionship. Bubba and Chad could fill that need, maybe.

She felt a lightness in her step as she considered how well Kyle Sherman was fitting into her life.

"I'LL BE DANGED," Bubba said. "Those are some nice houses for birds."

"Yeah, well, it passes the time." Kyle concentrated on slapping a coat of green paint on the roofs of five birdhouses. He'd reached the point where he crafted five at one time. This increased production, and he could always add individual touches in the details so they weren't identical.

"You sell many?"

"A few here and there." In fact, Kyle couldn't keep up with the demand. Mayzelle's sister ordered some for her gift shop, and Glenda at the Curly Q had told Dixie that she'd like to stock several for her customers.

Chad surveyed the line of birdhouses on the shelf. "You've found a nice hobby," he observed.

"Why don't you tell him your hobby," Bubba suggested.

Kyle took a swig of beer. It was a good bit stronger than the brand he bought at Bi-Lo.

"Well, I like working on my old Corvette," Chad said.

"That's not what I'm talking about," Bubba said.

"Wait a minute, I was getting interested in the Corvette," Kyle told them with a grin.

"No, it's his other hobby that will impress you," said Bubba.

"I'm with a volunteer infantry division of Confederate reenactors," Chad said. "We may have faced each other on the battlefield at Rivervale Bridge."

"No kidding," Kyle said.

"No kidding."

A slow smile spread across Kyle's face. "Cool."

"Yeah," Chad said. "Except that you were fighting on the wrong side." He was smiling as he said it, and Kyle grinned back at him.

"Let's take our beer down by the lake and talk about it," Kyle said. He was interested in whether the Confederate reenactors felt a bond as close as the one he had with his friends back in Ohio. He was eager to share his own story, and he was glad that Chad wanted to hear it.

They sat at the picnic table with Bubba's dog curled at their feet. Kyle hadn't kicked back like this since Rivervale Bridge, and it was good to be talking guy talk. Dixie was fun, and he liked how they tossed topics back and forth, but sometimes he was hungry for the kind of things men talk about.

"My family lost a lot of members in that war," Chad said as they watched the water spilling out of the artesian well and wending its way downhill to the lake. "Their surnames were Kershaw and Wood, Dawson, Browning and Honour. It was a terrible war in terms of how many Americans died, North and South."

Kyle said that he'd joined the reenactors because of his love of history and his wish to memorialize everyone who fought and died. "It really has nothing to do with who my great-great-great-grandfather was," he said.

"You know how we still feel about General William T. Sherman around here," Bubba said, not unkindly. "My great-grandfather cursed every time he heard his name. But that was a long time ago. And, Yankee, I like you." He punched Kyle's arm.

"Yeah," Chad chimed in, and then he told Kyle where his reenactor group met and how he often traveled long distances to reenactments. Like Kyle's group, Chad's donated net proceeds from their sponsored reenactments to historic preservation.

"You could visit a meeting sometime," Chad offered. "At least forty percent of our members are transplants from the North. You wouldn't feel out of place."

By the time they'd finished their beer, Kyle was sure he wouldn't. "I'd like that," he said.

They all stood. "Say, Kyle, those rocks need resetting around that well," Bubba said.

"I figure if I could make a waterfall to tumble over the rocks, it would be really pretty."

"I'm a bricklayer, and I can supply the mortar. How about if I drop by some Saturday and we see what we can accomplish."

"Great idea," Kyle said. "You, too, Chad?"

"Count me in."

Sharing a spirit of compatibility, the three of them went back to the workshop, where Kyle asked Bubba to hold one of the birdhouses steady while he glued on a perch. "Say, Kyle," Bubba said, squinting a bit. "Doesn't this bird palace look a lot like Dixie's new house?"

Kyle was amused. "You noticed," he said.

"Why, you've put in the dormer windows and even that funny little niche by the front door."

Kyle had taken his time over this particular birdhouse, a surprise for Dixie. Mayzelle had mentioned on the sly that Dixie's birthday was coming up soon.

"She's not supposed to see it until her birthday," Kyle said. "Don't tell her, okay?"

"Okay. She'll be pleased about it. Dixie does like pretty things."

Kyle sent Bubba on his way with one of his birdhouses for Katie. After they left, he went in the house and found Dixie coiling up the iron's cord. She'd ironed his uniform, and it hung on the stand beside her own clothes.

"I like Bubba, just as you said I would," he told her.

"That's good. How about if I invite him and Katie for dinner soon?"

"Go for it."

She'd tuned the radio to the classical-music station out of Columbia. It was playing a waltz, something elegant and Strausslike. He pulled her into dance position and swooped her into the hall.

"I didn't realize you could dance like this!" Dixie exclaimed.

"What else don't you know about me?" Her eyes were bright and she smelled of spray starch, which inexplicably turned him on.

"I don't have a clue whether you like turnips," Dixie said, matching him step for step as he twirled her toward the staircase. "Which I might serve in a salad when we have Bubba and Katie over."

"I'll try the turnips, but I can't promise anything."

"I'll call Katie and ask them for tomorrow night."

"Chad, too?"

"If you like."

"I like," he said, stopping suddenly and running his hand lower until he encountered warm flesh.

"You ready to make love?" Dixie asked as she nuzzled his neck.

"Maybe. Since we'll be busy tomorrow night."

She unbuttoned his shirt. "I'm busy right now. Why aren't you?"

As always, there was no resisting her. "Have you ever made love on an ironing board?" he asked playfully.

"*Eeew.* Think of something else."

He swung her into his arms and climbed the stairs with her à la Rhett Butler and Scarlett O'Hara, except that the staircase wasn't grand and Dixie was whooping with laughter. When he deposited her on the bed, she reached up and pulled him down on top of her. And then they were both very busy indeed.

Chapter Eight

The following Saturday morning was Dixie's birthday. She exclaimed at great length over Kyle's present of the birdhouse, which she loved, and fixed them a true Southern breakfast complete with eggs, sausage, grits and biscuits. Her grandmother called, her sister and Voncille, too. She and her relatives laughed a lot when they were on the phone, and they had so many things to say to each other that it was hard to hang up.

After she finished her conversation with Voncille, Kyle appeared in the kitchen doorway. "I'm considering what I'm going to do today. Do you have to work?"

"No, all's quiet on the real estate front."

"Nothing from Lana Pillsbry on that house you showed her?"

"Not a word. I'm worried. I hope she doesn't find something else."

"Hey," he said. "She'll buy it."

"There's many a slip 'tween the cup and the lip in this business."

"I'm supposed to go to Camden and tend to a couple of horses. It's your birthday, so why don't you ride along with me. If you haven't planned anything better, that is."

Dixie stood up. It was almost as if he'd been reading her mind; she wanted to spend the day with him. "Sounds great. I'll be ready in a jiff." She shot him a happy smile as she hurried upstairs to her bedroom and changed into jeans and a sweater.

When she came downstairs, Kyle was jingling his keys, impatient to be going.

"I could fix lunch," she said. "We could have a birthday picnic."

He glanced at his watch. "I won't be hungry for a long time after that humongous breakfast. We'll grab something to eat when we're ready." He slid a companionable arm across her shoulders as they walked toward the truck.

Their mood lightened even more once they were on the road with the greening trees whizzing past, the black pavement unfurling before them. As he drove, Kyle explained the work he'd been doing for Mac McGehee, the farrier who was still recovering from a stroke. "He won't be back to normal for a long time. Maybe he won't be well enough to work at all. He offered me a chance to buy his equipment, take over his customers."

"What about your business in Ohio?" Dixie asked.

"I spoke with Harry who's still covering for me. He's got it under control." Kyle didn't say anything more than that, and Dixie didn't press him for more details. She was reluctant to seem too eager for him to change his life around. He'd said he was considering a move to South Carolina, but she realized that any final decision in that direction should be made by Kyle alone.

When they arrived in Camden, Kyle drove through quiet streets to a stable on the outskirts of town, parking in the shade of an enormous willow oak. As soon as they were out of the truck, a short squat man stepped out of the paddock and hobbled toward them, greeting Kyle warmly.

"Jarvis Wilfield, this is Dixie Lee Smith," Kyle said, drawing her forward with an arm around her shoulders.

"We couldn't have managed without Kyle to help us out," Jarvis told Dixie, his eyes lighting up as he shook her hand. "He's a godsend."

Dixie murmured something appropriate and followed the men into the cool shadowy stable. In a stall toward the rear, a big roan was peering over the door.

"That's the one," Jarvis said, leading the way. Dixie inhaled the heady scents of hay and feed and horse while the two men led the roan outside. He was a sturdily built gelding, and Dixie followed them into the paddock.

"Old Dexter here is a fine horse," Jarvis said. "He works weddings, mostly. Local brides like to hire Dex and his surrey for their departure from the church, and he loves the duty. Trouble is, he threw a shoe the other day and we've got a big wedding coming up this weekend."

Kyle stroked Dexter's flank before bending to pick up the horse's foot. He inspected it carefully. "Not a problem," he said. "We'll set up my equipment and take care of it."

As Jarvis tied Dexter loosely to a fence rail, Kyle and Dixie went back to his truck where he opened the back hatch. "First the anvil," Kyle said. "Then the stand." Kyle placed the anvil carefully on the stand and directed Dixie to reach for two farrier's aprons hanging on hooks inside the truck. When they reentered the paddock, Dexter, waiting patiently, turned his head at their approach.

Dixie had always liked horses, but ever since her grandfather sold the pony he'd kept at the farm during her childhood, she hadn't had many chances to ride.

"Hello, Dexter," she said, wishing he could talk back. However, this horse was no chattery Mr. Ed. He blinked patiently, his long lashes dark and feathery, and whinnied softly as she stroked his face and rubbed his ears.

Kyle, acting very professional, ran his hand along Dexter's leg. Facing in the same direction as the horse, he bent so that his knees supported the horse's hoof. Dexter didn't seem to mind; he was more interested in whisking his tail back and forth to chase away a horsefly.

Dixie stood back and watched as Kyle efficiently scraped out the dirt packed between the hoof wall and the V-shaped pad toward the back of the hoof. "I might as well put you to work," Kyle said to Dixie. "You interested in trying this?"

Not one to be left out, she answered, "Sure!"

Kyle stepped aside so that she could move into position. As Kyle instructed, she picked Dexter's hoof up off the ground. Kyle handed her a metal brush. "Brush away the debris until the hoof is clean," he told her.

When Dixie had completed the task, she glanced up at Kyle, who was standing nearby. "Now what?"

"We change places," he said.

Dixie moved aside, and Kyle carefully used a knife to trim a good quarter of an inch from the edge of the hoof. He smoothed the hoof's edge with a metal file called a rasp. "I bet you didn't realize you were going to witness a horse's pedicure today, did you?"

She laughed. "Hey, it's my birthday. Amazing things could happen." She was thinking of that sale to Lana and what a great present it would be if Lana called today and told her she'd take the house.

Kyle turned the rasp over and used it to even out the bottom of the hoof. Then he left Jarvis to murmur encouraging words to Dexter before going to the truck and heating up the propane forge.

Staying well back from the work area, Dixie perched on a nearby stone wall.

"These flames heat to over 2000 degrees Fahrenheit," Kyle said. Muscles rippled in his arms as he readied his equipment. "Hand me that pair of tongs over there, will you?" He smiled at her, the sun glinting off his hair.

Holding the horseshoe with the tongs, Kyle placed it in the forge. Minutes later, when he opened the door, Dixie reeled from the blast of heat. Kyle carried the very hot shoe to the anvil for shaping. Kyle hammered the metal thin on one side, explaining that he was turning up the metal around the shoe's edges so that it wouldn't shift on the horse's foot.

Kyle had to return the shoe to the forge several times before the shape was perfect. When he was satisfied, he smoothed the edges on a power grinder. Back in the paddock, he bent down under the horse again and held the shoe against the hoof. As he kept the shoe in place, Kyle tapped nails through precut holes. "The angle of the nails is important," he said. "When it's right, the nail's point emerges through the hoof wall."

When all the nails were hammered in, Kyle set the foot on a metal stand and snipped off the nail tip. He smoothed their edges with the rasp and directed Dixie as she brushed on a clear sealer. Through it all, the horse stood quietly, an amused glint in his eyes as if entertained by the mysterious antics of humans.

"There, that's done," Kyle said. "Good boy, Dexter." He stroked the horse's neck.

Jarvis came out of the stable, all smiles. Together they led Dexter back to his stall, and Jarvis gave Dixie a carrot to feed him. Dexter seemed unaffected by his experience, and Jarvis seemed much relieved that no bride would be disappointed this weekend for lack of a proper conveyance for her wedding.

With Dexter properly shoed, Kyle forged corrective shoes for a Tennessee walker before trimming the hooves of a gentle mare who worked with a therapist for visually impaired children. By the time they were ready to leave, it was well past lunchtime. The hours had passed so quickly that Dixie had hardly noticed. She understood now why Kyle loved his work.

They bought a bucket of hot wings and a couple of Yoo-hoos at a local take-out place near the edge of town and stopped to eat a late lunch at a small picnic area off the highway. A lonely swamp stretched into the distance, the reeds along the shore waving gently in the wind. From a nearby cypress, a blue jay chided them for disturbing his territory. A lazy turtle ambled out from under the lone weeping willow and stared for a moment before drawing its head and feet back into his shell.

They spread their food and drinks on a circular concrete picnic table with a wide-angle view, polishing off the wings one by one.

"Now you have firsthand knowledge of what I do for a living," Kyle said. He smiled at her across the table.

Dixie reached for another piece of chicken. "I'm impressed with the way you relate to the animals," she said truthfully.

He picked up her hand and kissed it. "It meant a lot to have you with me today."

"I liked it, too," she replied, surprised that he'd say so.

"You'll come with me again sometime?"

Sometimes Kyle was so dear, like this morning when he gave her the clumsily wrapped birdhouse that he'd crafted just for her. "Far be it from me to shirk work of any kind," she said warmly. "Especially when there are hot wings involved."

This had been a perfect day, a wonderful birthday, and she wished it didn't have to end. Kyle must have been of the same mind, because as they were cleaning up the site, he said, "Say, Dixie. Have you ever made love under a weeping willow?"

She laughed, delighted that he'd suggest it. "No, but there's always a first time."

Kyle waggled his eyebrows at her and went to the truck to fetch a blanket. She helped him spread it under the tree, and he took her hand. "Dixie, Dixie," he murmured. "What am I going to do about you?"

"I have some indecent suggestions," she told him, arching her brows as he drew her close. He began to undress her, letting clothes fall where they would, and she crossed her arms across her chest.

"You're so beautiful," he said. "Let me see you." He took her arms and uncrossed them, exposing her to his gaze. Then slowly he undressed until they were naked together.

"We're like Adam and Eve," she said softly, and he smiled.

"Without the fig leaves."

The sunshine filtering through the filigree of branches bathed them in a delicate shimmering light, the breeze whispered on their bare skin. Kyle's eyes were dark and glinting with gold, and for a moment, she thought she divined a deeper emotion in their depths. She took a moment to marvel how love had flowed so easily into her life, taking its form in him. Her perception trembled on the verge of what she was ready to articulate, and she dared to hope that he was ready, too.

But he didn't speak. His arms went around her. It seemed natural to come together there, to hold each other in that cool, shadowy refuge as he drew her down to the blanket.

Caught up in the magic of the moment, all at once Dixie's senses opened like the blossom of a flower. Touching, tasting, inhaling his quickened breath; her heart racing, her throat vulnerable to his kisses, her mouth crushed against his. His hands cooling her hot breasts, his lips drawing her nipples deeply into his mouth. Her greediness for Kyle knew no bounds, and she was lost in a haze of passion. No, not lost but found, and it was so good, so right. When his heart shuddered against hers, she rose to meet him, her world imploding along with his.

Afterward, she lay with her lips in the hollow between his collarbone and throat, her eyes closed, realizing that she had never known such joy. When she opened her eyes, the late-afternoon sun had tinged the swamp with amber light and gilded the branches of the willow. The air was hushed around them, and it was as if they were the only people in the world. Dixie would have stayed there until the night enfolded them, but a chill twilight had begun to spread across the marsh, and they agreed that they must go.

Before they left, Kyle held Dixie in his arms for a long moment.

"Our lovemaking is like a communion of souls," he said. "We're special, Dixie. I never expected to find a woman as exciting as you."

"I never figured I'd find a man who could appreciate me."

He chuckled and slapped her lightly on the rump. "We'd

better get out of here before Lizard Man turns up. Didn't that guy who saw him have a bucket of fried chicken beside him on the car seat?"

Dixie laughed. "Yes, but all we have left are the bones of a bunch of chicken wings. I'm not too sure even Lizard Man would want those."

They gathered up the blanket and their picnic things, and Kyle took her hand as they walked back to the truck.

As Kyle drove toward home, it occurred to Dixie that her thirtieth birthday could turn into the kind of night on which a woman who has made up her mind to find a husband, maximized her chances and found the perfect man could expect a proposal of marriage. Maybe later they could walk down the dock and gaze at the stars, giving Kyle a chance to pop the question. Wrapped in a cocoon of pleasure and anticipation, she fantasized about the possibility on the drive back to Yewville.

When Kyle turned the truck into her driveway, a late-model gray sedan was parked outside the garage.

Disconcerted, Dixie thudded back to reality. "Whose car is that?" she asked.

Kyle didn't reply, though a peculiar expression washed across his face. It bespoke wariness, disbelief or worse.

Dixie sat forward a bit. "That car doesn't belong to any friends of mine," she said with definite foreboding. "And it doesn't look like a birthday present." As she spoke, a figure emerged from the shadows and walked smartly down the back steps. It was female in nature, wearing a charcoal business suit with no-nonsense dark pumps. And its handbag yapped.

"Oh, damn," Kyle said in pure disgust.

"Who is it?" Dixie asked as if she didn't know.

"Unfortunately, it's Andrea," he said. "And Twinkle."

"THERE NOW, Twinks," Andrea said as the little Yorkie lifted a leg against one of the newly transplanted dogwood saplings. "You're due for a treat." She tossed him a biscuit.

"So are we," Kyle said under his breath. "Apparently."

Dixie ignored this, giving every evidence that her mind was running in circles trying to figure out what the unannounced appearance of Kyle's former girlfriend meant. The woman was giving Dixie the once-over. No, make that a twice-over, going for three.

"Well, um, do come in," Dixie said politely, though this invitation brought forth daggers of indignance from Kyle's eyes, as in, "What's up with *this?*" Nevertheless, he was sure that Dixie was not going to let a stranger leave the premises without offering at least a glass of iced tea. He loved her for her hospitality—where would he be without it? This, however, might be over the top.

Twinkle lifted his head and sniffed the air. Kyle immediately realized that the dog was perking up to the familiar scent that told him there was something worth biting in the area. *Bingo!* Twinkle, beribboned topknot bouncing above his eyes, growled and aimed straight for Kyle's calf. Kyle jumped aside a mere second before the animal would have sunk his fangs into the skin.

"Up to his old tricks," Kyle muttered.

Andrea scooped Twinkle up and stuffed him into her purse. "Go to sleep. Twinks. It's been a long day," she said soothingly.

And getting even longer, Kyle thought.

Dixie held the back door open, and Andrea marched inside.

Kyle, wondering why Andrea got to use the back door same as any friend, followed the two women. At the moment, he wished he were anywhere else, but no one seemed to care.

"Andrea, you shouldn't have come here," he said when they were all congregated in Dixie's kitchen.

"I want to talk," Andrea said to Kyle, blinking in the light from the fluorescent fixture over the sink. "Since you wouldn't go home, I came to you instead."

Dixie hiked her brows at that. "Why don't we all sit down," she suggested as she began to pour tea from the unending supply in the pitcher.

After setting a glass in front of each of them, Dixie took her place beside Andrea. Kyle had compared the two women in his mind, and now he could do it in person. Though Andrea's dark hair was usually sleek and well styled, tonight it drooped over her forehead, hanging in her eyes. Her suit fit too tightly across the bust and hips, indicating that she'd gained weight since Kyle had seen her last. Dixie, on the other hand, was blond perfection in blue jeans worn with a form-fitting sweater the shade of daffodils but with a bit of a dry brown leaf stuck to the back.

"Why are you really here, Andrea?"

"Like I said. To talk to you." The way Andrea was so critically studying Dixie revealed the real truth, which was that she was eager to find out what kind of woman had won his heart.

"Where are you staying?"

Andrea tossed her hair back. "You can recommend a good motel, right?"

"You won't find a room at the Magnolia, that's the only local place," Kyle told her. He was more than familiar with how fast the Magnolia's available rooms were usually taken on weekends.

"I saw another possibility on the way into town. The sign advertised rooms for six dollars an hour."

"Not a good idea," Kyle said hastily. "On the other hand, you could try Florence. It's a thirty-five-mile drive."

Andrea stared uncomprehendingly. "That's way too far."

"I, um," Dixie began, ignoring his warning glance.

"Dixie," he cautioned, but she avoided his eyes.

"I suppose you could sleep here," Dixie finished against his will. So much for communion of the spirit. She'd switched off on her end, obviously.

"Dixie, are you out of your mind?" he bellowed.

Andrea spared Dixie a look of gratitude or maybe it was some other emotion, he wasn't sure. The only clear thing was that the two of them were now a closed circuit and he wasn't in their loop.

"You *could* bunk in the playhouse," Dixie said to Andrea.

A faint smile touched Andrea's lips. "Oh, that little doll house? I peeked in the window when I first arrived. It's surely too small."

"Well, back to the spare bedrooms," Dixie said, valiantly trying again. "I haven't set up the extra bed yet, it's just a mattress and box springs on the floor, but you're welcome to it. Isn't she, Kyle?"

He was not under any circumstances going to sleep with Dixie in her room with his ex listening on the other side of the thin walls. He tried to come up with alternate arrangements that wouldn't require him to move to another bed, but there weren't any.

"*I'll* sleep in the playhouse," he said.

Dixie tilted her head as if perplexed, and Kyle supposed it was too much for her to understand. She regarded sex between two consenting adults as only natural and right, so chances were that if it occurred to her that Andrea might hear or see something, she wouldn't care. And there was always the possibility that Dixie was the sort who would like to show off how sexually compatible they were with a stellar performance, complete with bed knockings and intensified moans in hopes of running Andrea off ASAP. Women were like that sometimes.

He stood to leave. "See you in the morning." By mistake he bumped against Andrea's purse on the way out the back door, dislodging Twinkle. The dog growled menacingly and chased him, but Kyle managed to slam the screen door between them in the nick of time. He hoped the dog got a snoutful of plastic mesh.

Kyle glumly stuffed his hands down in his pockets and headed for the playhouse. By the time he was lying on the cot, the only lights lit in the big house were upstairs.

He'd much rather be resting beside Dixie, the TV on in the background as he stroked her hair back from her forehead with one hand and explored her sweet curves with the other. He dreamed about never having to sleep apart from her again, if that were actually possible.

It was an hour or so before he was surprised by the application of two cold feet to his warm ones. He woke with a start.

"Dixie?"

"Well, who else would it be? I wish I'd worn my warm nightgown, though, seeing as how it's a little chilly in here."

"We could warm this place up real fast."

"That's what I'm banking on. I brought a half bottle of merlot to help us out."

He hitched himself up onto one elbow and made room for her and the cold bottle between them. By now something else was between them, as well, rendering Dixie most appreciative.

"Maybe we could leave the wine for later," she said, closing her cold hands around him.

"Damn right," he said. "Have you ever made love on a balance beam?"

"Very funny," Dixie murmured as she slid her leg over his.

He didn't remember the wine until much later, but by then, they were out of the mood for it.

ON MONDAY MORNING, Dixie was enjoying her second cup of coffee in the break room at the Yewville Real Estate office, and Mayzelle was listening to her recap of Saturday night's Andrea appearance.

"She brought her nasty little dog?" Mayzelle asked, all ears. "It tried to bite Kyle?"

"Yes, and at first, Kyle seemed primed to kick that animal clear out of the house," Dixie said.

"Kyle wouldn't harm anything if his life depended on it," Mayzelle said, bending down to stroke one of Fluffy's silky ears.

"Well, he must have hurt Andrea pretty seriously," Dixie retorted. "Otherwise why would she travel more than five hundred miles to have a word with him?"

Mayzelle pursed her lips, considering. "Just in case he's made an awful mistake and feels like correcting it?"

"She's bound to be sadly disappointed. He's fixing to move down here. Or at least he's making noises about it."

"He's wanting to be near *you*," Mayzelle pointed out approvingly.

"That, too." This knowledge was a source of comfort.

"What does Andrea look like?"

"They say people start to resemble their dogs. Andrea doesn't. Just the opposite, in fact—she's all sleek dark hair and a long skinny face." Despite Dixie's prior imaginings, Kyle's ex wasn't at all voluptuous, and she didn't wear dangly earrings. Dixie wasn't sure about the see-through underwear, but she'd been relieved to discover that Andrea's voice wasn't sexy but pitched in a register slightly higher than a fire alarm.

Mayzelle sat up straight and frowned. "Do I look like Fluffy?" she asked anxiously with a doubtful glance at her overweight poodle.

"Not at all, Mayzelle," Dixie said, being generous. "Your hairdo is way more trendy. Plus, the color is back to Desert Dream, and it's very becoming."

"You're sure?"

"Absolutely."

"I'm surprised you didn't throw Andrea out right away," Mayzelle said. "I would have."

"My mama raised me to help people out when I can. Andrea's a woman in a strange town with no decent motel rooms likely to be available. I mean, I've had boyfriends that did me wrong. I went to some lengths to express my unhappiness about it, and that's apparently what she's doing. I wouldn't care to be tossed out into the night if I were Andrea."

"Dixie—"

"Now, never you mind, Mayzelle. I think what I think, and in my opinion, I'm better off to let Andrea have her say with Kyle. Then we'll be rid of her for good."

"You do seem sure of yourself," Mayzelle told her.

"I'd say I'm over those self-esteem problems," Dixie said, though in her mind she'd never had any.

"You go, girl!"

They exchanged grins.

"What did everyone do at your house yesterday? I'm trying to imagine what it must have been like around there."

"Kyle went to Camden, an easy out. I attended church as usual, then Sunday dinner at Memaw's, and I threw in a couple of loads of laundry when I got home. Andrea kept bugging me about when Kyle was coming back, and when he didn't show up by dark, she asked me if I wanted to go out for a drink."

"Did you?"

"No, I pointed her in the direction of the cream cake in the fridge and left to visit Voncille, Skeeter and the kids."

"What about Kyle?"

"He was asleep in the playhouse when I got back from Vonnie's. I joined him."

Mayzelle laughed. "And stayed all night."

"You got it." The bed was hardly big enough for one person, much less a couple, and now she'd slept in it with Kyle for two nights in a row. But they'd managed. Oh, how they had managed. Her neck was still stiff from the effort of making love with her head hanging off the end of the mattress last night. Kyle had snickered and said that they would have been better off to do it standing up, but Dixie pointed out that since he was so tall and the ceiling so low, he would have been the one with the stiff neck in that case.

"So what's happening now?"

"Kyle is going to talk to her."

Mayzelle tossed her foam cup in the trash can. "When you get home today, I bet Andrea is gone."

"When I get home, she'd better be."

Dixie and Mayzelle were both laughing as Dixie gathered up her papers for her appointment with the Maine coon man.

THAT MORNING, shortly after Dixie left for work, Kyle began scrubbing their breakfast eggs off the forks, framing his upcoming discussion with Andrea in his head. While he was cleaning up, Andrea floated downstairs, trailing several yards of pale blue chiffon and cradling Twinkle under one arm.

"Coffee?" Kyle offered, trying not to see through her negligee, though that was clearly the whole point.

Andrea accepted a mug, which was good. He'd never been able to have a meaningful conversation with her before her morning caffeine fix.

"What's to eat?" she asked with a yawn.

"Eggs in the refrigerator, bagels in the freezer."

"We could eat breakfast together."

"Think again."

"And then I need to get online and send some e-mails."

"There's a Wi-Fi connection in Dixie's home office. Feel free." He'd postpone their discussion until after she'd sent her e-mails because then Andrea would have no excuse to stay. She'd pack and leave.

Kyle tossed a sponge into the dish drainer and flicked on the garbage disposal. Andrea bent down to peer into the refrigerator, thereby revealing a rounded expanse of breast. Despite his best intentions to get their discussion over with, he shut off the disposal and beat a hurried retreat for the door, unwilling to be coaxed into betraying Dixie by Andrea's intentional exposure of body parts. That wasn't his only concern by this time. Twin-

kle had started to yip, never a good sign. Once Andrea put him
on the floor, it was one second to lunging mode.

"Andrea, I have to go out. There's a truck stop on the bypass called Dolly's, and I'll meet you there for lunch." Strictly
speaking, Kyle didn't have to go anywhere right now, but it
seemed advisable to vacate the premises. Dolly's was a public
place, and Andrea would be less likely to cause a ruckus with
other people around.

"Kyle?"

Ignoring Andrea's plaintive voice, Kyle kept walking to his
truck and subsequently scratched out of the driveway. Dolly's
wasn't the best choice for a heart-to-heart with Andrea, since
the place was frequented by easy women, but as he'd discovered one day recently, the cook there made a great burger.
Besides, he didn't care to risk parading his ex-girlfriend past
Kathy Lou and the regulars at the Eat Right Café. There was
enough gossip about his romance with Dixie without adding
Andrea to the mix.

"WHAT DO I HAVE TO DO to get you back?" Andrea asked, her
hands curved around the bun of a giant butter burger, the
house specialty.

Kyle thought this over, which took approximately half a
nanosecond. "Why would you want me when you've seen fit
to break up with me four—no, make that five—times?"

"We're so good together, Kyle," Andrea said matter-of-
factly. He had the idea that she, in her CPA fashion, had toted
up a row of figures and come up with the answer: KYLE. She
didn't seem to attach much, if any, emotion to her claim to
him. Nor had she ever, he realized belatedly.

"We're not good together at all," he objected, nudging a

fallen French fry away from the edge of the table. "We fight, we make up. We trot along at a steady pace for a while and then we slam up against a stone wall. The reality is that we have almost nothing in common."

"Sex," Andrea said, offering the word up like a prayer, though it was almost lost in the blast of loud twangy music wailing from speakers directly over their heads.

The truth was that Kyle hadn't liked what went on between the sheets with Andrea nearly as much as he enjoyed his rollicking sex life with Dixie. Andrea wasn't inventive or imaginative. She approached the sex act as something that people had to do, like homework, or—or paying taxes. Fill out this form, sign that one, and lo, someone has a climax, which should hold both of them until the next payment is due.

"WE LIKE SEX," Andrea repeated loudly just as the music ended, and several patrons turned to stare curiously.

For the first time, Kyle noticed that Andrea's smile, which come to think of it, only appeared briefly now and then, was bracketed by frown lines that remained when her face was in repose. He forced himself back to the issue at hand.

Somehow it didn't seem proper to tell Andrea that he'd found someone who was a whole lot better at lovemaking. "Sex isn't all there is to a relationship," he said. He forcibly pulled his gaze away from Andrea's low neckline, which featured a narrow red ruffle coasting down into her cleavage.

"We have mutual friends," she said, as if that should give him pause. He recognized the mulish expression that always accompanied such arguments.

Before Kyle had a chance to respond, Andrea ticked a bunch of names off on her buttery fingers. "Rod and Allison, and Steve. I introduced him to you, remember. Elliott and Margo. Jan Cahoun, when she isn't at her place in Colorado."

"Agreed, but there's also something called commonality of interest. For instance, I'm bored with that theater group you're so fond of." Most of their mutual friends were in it.

"But—"

He waved away her objection. "Boring. *Boring.* It's always the same actors in a different play. I don't like getting gussied up in a tux, yet you love attending formal opening night of the season and parading me around like I'm Twinkle on a leash. We disagree about politics, food, music and my work. Frankly, Andrea, I'm amazed that we lasted as long as we did."

"You know the last play of the season is coming up, and I'm counting on you as my escort."

"I don't care to watch the same person who starred as Annie in *Annie Get Your Gun* playing a slightly long-in-the-tooth Nellie Forbush in *South Pacific.*"

"Shawna is one of my best friends."

Kyle said nothing.

Andrea took another bite of her burger and chewed, meanwhile overtly checking out the big-haired woman in a sequined tube top who was moving among customers in the back room where the pool table stood.

"Is that what Southern belles wear around here?" Andrea asked after she'd swallowed. Her gaze followed the woman, who laughed uproariously and pinched a guy's cheek as they watched.

The woman was likely one of the floozies imported from across some state line or other for temporary work. "Uh, I don't know," Kyle said. "You shouldn't have come here, Andrea."

Andrea, returning her attention to matters at hand, poked

at the slab of tomato resting on her lettuce. "I had to make sure you're all right," she said self-righteously.

"I'm as all right as I've ever been."

"Maybe we need couples counseling. Shawna knows this woman—"

"As I have already told you more than once, it's over. You like the idea of counseling, you go right ahead." He again cautioned himself to hold his temper.

"Tell me about Dixie," Andrea said. "What is she to you?"

There were all sorts of ways that Kyle could have replied to that. Dixie was a sweet fragrance borne upon a gentle southern wind, a balm to his soul. She was sunshine, she was rain, she was earth, water and sky. She was, in fact, everything.

"We're a couple," he said, a simple declaration. "I don't know what I'd do without her." This was, he realized as he spoke, the truth.

Andrea appeared more than a bit flustered. "And you met how?"

"It's really none of your business, Andrea."

"I'm only looking out for you."

"Well, go look out for someone else. Falling in love is something that a person generally can handle on his own." He wasn't quite sure he'd said that until a light went out in Andrea's eyes and her face turned ashen.

"You—you're in love with Dixie?"

He waited a long moment, turning the idea over in his mind. In love with Dixie? Could it be true?

"Yeah," he said. "I guess I am."

"I see," Andrea said quietly.

"You've met her. You can see why I care about her." He took pity on Andrea, though he was certain by this time that they would have broken up for good whether he'd found Dixie or not.

"You wouldn't have to love her."

But I want to. "Leave it, Andrea. Nothing can come of pursuing this. Of pursuing *me,*" he corrected. "Take on the next plane home and have a nice life." He spoke as kindly as he could.

Her eyes suddenly filled with tears. "Oh, Kyle," she said brokenly, his cue to leave, but before he could escape, she jumped up and bolted toward the door, her short skirt flouncing above her knees. This momentary glimpse of a long expanse of leg—he was only human—meant that he didn't realize she'd left her purse on the floor until she was backing her rental car out of the parking lot.

Twinkle poked his nose out, sniffed, and eyed Kyle's pants leg. Kyle responded by shoving what was left of Andrea's butter burger in on top of the dog and snapping the flap of the purse down tight.

He grabbed the purse and headed for the door. There was something about carrying a woman's handbag that made a man want to mince along, but he fought it. It helped that he was wearing his work boots. A pert bespangled woman eyed the purse he was carrying. "You out for some fun this afternoon? Both ways?"

He kept walking.

Kyle figured that the half patty of hamburger meat might keep Twinkle's teeth occupied until they arrived back at the house. If not, he could probably bid a fond goodbye to this brand-new pair of Dockers.

Chapter Nine

Wouldn't you know that Leland Porter would insist that Dixie take possession of the cat on the very day that the worst spring thunderstorm in years decided to roll through the South Carolina Piedmont. And that the cat, a long-haired, white-bibbed gray tabby called Muffin, was smart enough to work her way out of the cardboard box that they'd pressed into service as a cat carrier. And would hop up next to the back window of Dixie's car and meow piteously the whole way back to her house.

Dixie spotted no sign of Andrea's rental car or Kyle's truck when she drove up to the house and into the garage. No sign of any people whatsoever. Dixie wished for the umpteenth time that the previous owners of her place had seen fit to attach the garage to the kitchen by a breezeway. Maybe that could be a building project for the future. Right now, she needed to convey Muffin to the house if the cat wasn't to spend the rest of the day crouching in the back of the Mustang. Anyway, Dixie wanted to show Muffin her new home.

Dixie leaned into the back of the car to take hold of Muffin.

Only the cat's front paws had been declawed, and Muffin demonstrated a perverse disposition to deliver mighty kicks with her back legs. Somehow, in a flurry of fur and accompanied by wails befitting a banshee, Dixie managed to haul Muffin from the car.

She dashed through the rain, the cat squalling and kicking, and tried the back door, which she never locked. On this day, however, someone had locked it, and she suspected that the culprit was Andrea, to whom she'd given a set of keys last night. Andrea had frowned when Dixie informed her that the back door always remained unlocked, and Dixie, tired of the conversation anyway, had tossed her the extra set of keys.

With rainwater sluicing uncomfortably down the back of her neck and probably shrinking her new dry-cleanable suit, which she'd donned that morning to impress Andrea that she was a real businesswoman, too, Dixie tried to summon her wits about her. Kyle might have left his own set of keys in the playhouse, and she could use his to get in the door.

"Bear with me," she said to Muffin. She didn't dare set the cat down, seeing as how Muffin didn't seem overly enthusiastic about her recent change in ownership. Leland had assured her that Maine coon cats were "gentle, sweet and calm." All except this one.

There was nothing to do but to run out to the playhouse with Muffin tucked under her arm like a football, grab Kyle's house keys off the hook where he'd left them and sprint back to the house.

She'd no sooner stepped inside the door and set Muffin down with the admonition to "wait right there while I get a towel and dry both of us off," when a beribboned ball of brown fur rocketed out of the pantry and set up a barking alarm that could have wakened half the dead in Yewville Cemetery.

Twinkle. Why hadn't she thought of him?

Well, because Andrea customarily carried the Yorkie around in her purse, and Andrea's rental car was missing, presumably parked wherever Andrea was at the moment, and therefore her dog shouldn't be around, either. A perfectly logical assumption, though there was no logical way of explaining this to Muffin.

Muffin, uttering one of her banshee yowls, launched herself into orbit. One of her back claws shredded the right foot of Dixie's new panty hose in transit.

The dog took off after the cat, and Dixie followed both. Through the hall, past the sewing room, into the living room and, from there, a mad dash upstairs. Muffin managed to stay in front of Twinkle, but the dog was not to be deterred. A flutter of fur, both Maine coon and Yorkie, drifted in their wake.

By the time Dixie made her way to the second story, Twinkle was jumping and barking, jumping and barking. His ecstasy at having something fun to chase propelled him from the master bedroom to the guest room to the tiny hall closet. Where Muffin had disappeared to Dixie could not figure.

"Muffin? Muffin?" she called, wary of what Twinkle might do if the cat actually reappeared. To forestall any further attack on the part of the Yorkie, Dixie lured him downstairs with a hot dog from a new packet in the refrigerator, though he seemed less than interested. She shoved his water dish inside the pantry, tossed the frankfurter on the floor and slammed Twinkle inside. Then she went to find the cat.

The cat, however, seemed to have disappeared altogether.

A search of closets, under her bed, the bathroom and the linen closet produced nothing except the desiccated body of a cockroach left behind by the previous owner.

She really ought to do some spring cleaning around here. Maybe she could start next week.

Dixie sank down on the overstuffed chair in the corner of her bedroom. She wondered where Kyle and Andrea had gone. *Kyle and Andrea,* she repeated in her head. *I don't much like the sound of those words in such proximity.*

At least they'd taken their separate cars, which seemed like a good sign. Then again, was it?

KYLE CAREENED his truck into Dixie's driveway, unsure what to expect. He'd dropped Twinkle off earlier before running the truck by Smitty's for an oil change. That had seemed like as good a way as any to spend the afternoon. Andrea's sedan wasn't parked in the driveway, and he assumed she'd gone for a drive or something to settle her nerves. He wondered when she'd start to miss Twinkle.

His heart was gladdened by the sight of Dixie's Mustang sitting in its usual place in the garage. He bounded up the steps to the house, found the door unlocked and heard Twinkle whining in the pantry.

"Dixie?"

No answer. She had to be here, though. He hadn't shut Twinkle in the pantry, and Andrea never would.

"Dixie? Honey?"

He heard a muffled noise from above and took the stairs two at a time. Dixie was huddled in the big chair in the dormer of her bedroom, a tissue pressed to her nose.

"Dixie, what's wrong?" He knelt beside her.

"Everything. Andrea, that awful dog and now Muffin is missing."

"Muffin?"

"My new cat. And you were gone."

"I'm here now." As for the rest of it, he was pretty sure Andrea would be departing soon.

"Tell me about Muffin," he said, searching for a safe topic.

"Leland had to leave town, so I brought Muffin home today and Andrea's purse dog tried to eat her."

"Better he should eat the cat than my ankle," Kyle muttered.

"What?" Dixie said.

"Nothing. I don't believe that dog could eat a cat, he's so tiny. Most cats could devour him in one bite."

"This cat has no claws. She couldn't hold him down long enough to eat him, more's the pity."

He slid his arm around Dixie, surreptitiously flicking a stray sequin off the back of his hand before she spotted it. "Let's you and me go out to dinner, what do you say?" That should cheer her up.

"It's raining, my hair's a mess and we have leftover ham casserole in the refrigerator."

Experience had taught him that Dixie didn't like to waste food, so he dropped the going-out-to-dinner idea. Besides, he loved ham casserole.

"Your hair will dry as pretty as ever. I'll make it clear to Andrea that she has to eat someplace else."

"Did you make anything else clear today?" Dixie asked, slanting a sideways look at him.

"She understands there's no resuming the relationship," he said. It hadn't been easy, and he didn't like to make women cry. Plus, he'd had to drive home with that fool dog making sounds like a food processor as he scarfed up the hamburger in the bottom of Andrea's purse.

"If that's the case, I guess everything will be back to normal around here soon." Dixie smiled a watery smile, and he kissed her temple.

"I sure hope so," Kyle said. "Now, get into some dry clothes. When you come downstairs, I'll open a bottle of wine."

"Okay." She gave him her hand, and he pulled her up. She began to jettison the wet clothes, which was why Kyle didn't leave as he'd planned. Dixie stripped all the way down to nude and started reclothing herself from the bottom up. First she shimmied into a pair of lace panties, pulled the matching bra out of a drawer and decided against it. Her breasts were round and firm as she shrugged into a sweatshirt, and Kyle couldn't pull his gaze away.

"Anything wrong?" Dixie asked.

Before he could answer, Andrea's car drove up. Hearing it, Dixie joined him at the bedroom window. The storm had abated and the sky was clearing.

"Don't worry, I'll handle this," he said, turning toward the door.

"Not so fast. Milo's truck is following right behind her."

"Milo? Why is he here?"

"Don't ask me."

They reached the kitchen in time to greet Andrea as she came in through the back door. Twinkle erupted in a new spate of barking, and Andrea immediately went to the pantry and liberated him. She scooped the dog up in her arms, glowering at Kyle.

Twinkle started barking again at the approach of Milo and his companion, a small puppy. Not that the pup was walking willingly. She obviously was not yet trained to the leash, and Milo was dragging her behind him like a wagon.

"Oh, he's got Minnie Pearl's daughter," Dixie said, clearly entranced. She went to the door.

"Minnie Pearl? Who's that?" Kyle asked, mystified.

"Bubba's coon dog," Dixie answered.

"Dixie?" Milo called as he approached. When he reached the screen door, he held up his hand to shade his eyes from the sun, which was now peeking though the clouds. "May I come in?"

Dixie sighed. "Why not. It seems as if everyone else in all creation is here."

Andrea moved to the far side of the kitchen, dropping her aloof and chillingly polite manner to study Milo and his companion. Twinkle kept squirming to get down, and the puppy was wagging her tail. She trotted over to Andrea on a leash that pulled out of a handle.

"Your Yorkie seems inspired to get to know Starbright better," Milo offered. He smiled at Andrea, and she stopped frowning.

"Your dog's name is Starbright?" she asked.

"Yup."

"Why, mine is named Twinkle. Isn't that a coincidence!" Andrea set the Yorkie down beside the pup. They were about the same size and immediately started sniffing at each other.

"Milo, why are you here?" Dixie asked.

Her former boyfriend seemed momentarily disconcerted but recovered quickly. "I came to apologize for the other night. I shouldn't have, well, lost control of myself like I did."

Andrea perked up, glancing from Milo to Dixie, who blushed slightly. "Oh, that's all right, Milo," Dixie said.

"It was just the stars and moon and the night and all. It reminded me of times gone by. But I didn't intend to make any trouble between the two of you."

"What are you talking about?" Andrea asked.

"Don't ask," warned Kyle.

Dixie glanced at Kyle, waiting to see if he was going to reply to Milo or if she should.

He took the lead. "It's okay, Milo. We're over it, aren't we, Dixie?"

"Over *what?*" asked Andrea. "Twinkle, stop that, it's not nice." Twinkle was checking out Starbright's nether end.

"Nothing," Kyle said.

"I'm glad there's no hard feelings. Let's shake on it." Milo held out his hand.

"First time I ever saw two men shake hands over nothing," Andrea said disdainfully.

"It wasn't exactly nothing," Dixie explained. "But it's nothing right now."

The dogs had aligned themselves face-to-face, and Starbright began to lick Twinkle's muzzle. "Will you look at that," marveled Andrea. "They're playing kissy face."

Kyle would bet that Starbright's affection owed less to true love than to the flavor of hamburger that no doubt lingered around Twinkle's mouth. He figured the less said about anything the better, wishing everyone would leave so he could enjoy some much-needed alone time with Dixie.

"I don't believe I got your name," Andrea said to Milo. She seemed to be regarding him favorably, and he brightened under her scrutiny.

"Andrea Ludovici, this is Milo, uh," Kyle said, forgetting Milo's last name.

"Milo Dingle," Milo said, taking in Andrea's low ruffled neckline and the shapeliness of her legs as revealed by her short skirt. "How do you do?"

Kyle almost laughed. If Dixie had married Milo, she would have been Dixie Dingle. Unless she was one of those modern women who would insist on keeping her birth name, which could be the case.

"I've had better days," Andrea said to Milo. Her eyes were by this time only slightly reddened from crying. She had moved closer to him and was twiddling with a strand of her hair, a habit that used to drive Kyle nuts.

"What do you say we take the dogs for a walk and you can tell me about it," Milo suggested.

Dixie cocked her head in surprise at this unexpected move on Milo's part, but Andrea wasted no time taking Milo up on his offer. "I'll get Twinkle's leash," she said. She ran upstairs.

"She's not from around here, is she?" Milo asked while Andrea was out of the room.

"No, she's just visiting," Kyle said.

"She's not—you're not—" Milo cast a puzzled glance at the ceiling, above which they could hear Andrea rummaging in the guest room. "It's okay for me to ask her out, right?"

Thank you, God, Kyle thought. "Absolutely," he said.

When Andrea reappeared, she'd changed from her dress into jeans and a checked blouse, and she'd pushed her hair back and secured it with a banana clip. The casual hairdo was out of character for her, but it did change her image to younger and more hip. She no longer looked like a case study in uptight.

"Shall we?" Andrea said to Milo, who seemed to have eyes only for her. Kyle had never seen a woman's personality change so fast; one minute she was an aggrieved party, and now she was walking across the room with a new and enticing wiggle to her hips. Kyle suddenly began to suspect that all along, Andrea's unpleasant personality traits might have been born of her determination to cement him into the relationship. He didn't necessarily like what this said about him, but he wasn't in the mood to contemplate it at the moment.

Milo held the door for her, and Andrea said sweetly to Dixie and Kyle, "Don't wait up for me."

It was five-thirty in the afternoon. "You're going back to Ohio," Kyle said.

Andrea shook her head. "I'm hoping to avail myself of Dixie's hospitality for a bit longer. I couldn't get a flight back tonight."

"Wait a minute," Kyle said, anger rising to the surface on a mere moment's provocation.

"Kyle," Dixie said, a restraining hand on his arm.

"She's leaving," Kyle retorted. Milo's gaze flicked from one of them to the other in confusion.

"Another night won't make that much difference," Dixie murmured in her most conciliatory fashion. Kyle was surprised, since Dixie obviously wanted Andrea gone as much as he did.

"I'll leave in the morning," Andrea said chirpily. "First thing."

Kyle was silent, glowering; Dixie remained gracious. "Fine," she said.

"Milo? Ready?" Andrea favored him with her most winning smile, and Milo followed her out the door.

Kyle eyed Dixie. "Are you out of your mind?"

"No, but what's one more night? When she was leaving the house anyway? I'm ready for together time, just the two of us."

Andrea and Milo were disappearing down the driveway, tromping through puddles that would surely ruin her pricey flats. Dixie opened the refrigerator door and took out the ham casserole. "I'll make a salad and you can heat this in the micro," she said.

"That sounds good to me," he replied. He slid his arms around her from the back and drew her close. His hands moved under her sweatshirt and circled her breasts. The nipples rose to his touch, and he thanked his lucky stars that she was so responsive.

Dixie swiveled in his arms as his hands slid lower to cup her lush curves. She turned her face upward for a kiss.

"And after dinner, what?" he said, barely able to talk. He was so into her it wasn't even funny. He ate, drank and thought Dixie Lee Smith; she was the dream woman of all time. He'd tell her this right now, but she was talking. What she said next reminded him exactly why she held such an important place in his heart.

"We can take the canoe out and paddle around the lake in the moonlight."

"I had something far more interesting in mind."

"My sentiments exactly. I need to ask you something."

"Shoot." He grinned down at her, feeling loopy.

"Have you ever tried to make love in a canoe, Kyle?"

"That'll work," he said, all but moaning with the pleasure of anticipation.

It took them only twenty minutes to heat and eat dinner, both of them wondering why they even bothered.

THEY HAD NO TROUBLE dropping the canoe down from its sling in the garage. They encountered no difficulties when launching it into the lake. Making love was a different story, however.

Dixie dissolved in laughter a few times while Kyle was trying to remove her clothes. Once he managed to tip the canoe so far to the right that they almost capsized. When they finally achieved their goal, no lovemaking could have been more beautiful. The stars above reflected in the shimmery surface of the lake, the lights from the house beamed a mellow glow over the dock and beyond, the singsong of crickets resounded from the reeds along the shore. Afterward, they lay quietly in the canoe for a long time, murmuring so their voices wouldn't carry back to the house in case Milo and Andrea had returned.

There was no sign of them when they tethered the canoe at the end of the dock. Milo's manly truck was still parked in the driveway, but the rental car was gone. Twinkle was nowhere in sight when Dixie and Kyle let themselves into the house and hurried upstairs to Dixie's bedroom. They cuddled in Dixie's double bed, falling asleep almost right away.

During the night Dixie kept her ears tuned for Andrea, but she never heard her. She was curious as to what could have happened to those two, but she didn't fear foul play. As she well knew, Milo would let no harm come to any woman under his protection. Maybe they'd opted for a wild night out in Florence. They could have started drinking there and decided not to drive home. Or maybe—

It didn't really matter. She was comfortable in her own bed. Kyle was beside her. And all was right with her world.

The next morning, which was Dixie's day off, Andrea and Twinkle wandered in through the back door as Dixie and Kyle were eating waffles.

"Hello, all," Andrea said. She was still wearing the jeans and checked shirt of the day before, but she'd lost the banana clip. Her hair needed brushing.

Without saying another word, Andrea continued on upstairs.

"Andrea?" Dixie called. "Are you all right?" What she really wanted to know was Andrea's time of departure so she and Kyle could plan a celebration.

"I've got a pounding headache. Too many melon sours at the Pee Dee Saloon." This was the in crowd's favorite bar in Florence.

"There's aspirin in the hall bath medicine cabinet," Dixie called out.

Andrea mumbled something, and Twinkle, released from his leash, came racing down the stairs. He was in full pursuit of Muffin, who hadn't shown her face around the house since Dixie brought her home.

Kyle and Dixie leaped up at the same time. Muffin stopped, stood her ground outside the sewing room, and hissed and spat. This didn't deter Twinkle, who one-upped the cat by yapping and growling and snapping in a way that would have been cartoonish if it hadn't posed a danger.

"You get Twinkle," Dixie yelled. "I'll grab Muffin." Dixie had no idea where the cat, who seemed terrified for her life, had been hiding all this time.

"I'd rather *you* get Twinkle," Kyle said, lunging for the dog. He managed to curve his hands around the dog's sleek little body, but Twinkle instantly wiggled free and raced full speed around the living room. In the meantime, Muffin had stopped yowling and jumped toward the back of the couch, where her lack of front claws caused her to fall to the floor, scrambled up and rocketed to the kitchen where she vaulted to the top of the counter. Unfortunately, she knocked a bottle of Karo Syrup to the floor, breaking it in the process. Syrup began to ooze under the refrigerator and toward the table and chairs.

"Where is Andrea?" Dixie shouted. "Can't she control her dog?"

"Sounds like she's throwing up," Kyle informed her, angling his head toward the stairs.

Dixie heard the unmistakable sound of retching. Right now she didn't have time to deal with that. She approached Muffin warily. "Nice kitty. Nice Muffin."

"Can you name her something else? Like Godzilla?" Kyle asked.

He had a point. The cat's fur was fluffed in the manner of someone who had stuck a finger into an electric socket. Her eyes blazed green fire. Her whiskers stuck straight out like daggers. Dixie would be crazy to pick up an animal who appeared so fearsome.

She picked her up anyway. Immediately Muffin sagged and shrank into a helpless little fur piece with no bones. The cat's eyes closed, and as Dixie hiked her higher on her shoulder, Muffin began to emit a cautious purr.

"I'm taking Muffin into the sewing room," Dixie said over the Yorkie's barking and growling.

"You're leaving me with *him?*" Kyle said incredulously from the dining room, where he'd cornered Twinkle.

"You bet." Dixie retreated behind a closed door and listened to the racket while she sat and cuddled Muffin.

"Stop it, you dumb dog!" shouted Kyle. "Get over here. No, not over here, over there. *Stop* it!"

Dixie buried her face in Muffin's long fur. "You must be hungry, you poor thing. You missed your welcome-home meal because of that nasty dog."

Muffin purred louder and began to knead Dixie's thigh with her clawless front paws. There was something comforting about holding the cat in her lap. *I could get used to this,* Dixie told herself.

"Got him!" Kyle yelled in triumph on the other side of the door. Dixie heard a scrabbling of feet and then nothing else.

"Kyle?"

"It's okay. I'm banishing Attila to the garage."

"Do that," Dixie murmured as Muffin butted her head against her idle hand. She figured that was cat language for "keep petting me," so she did. Frantic barking ensued from the general direction of the garage. Dixie wondered when the next plane left for Ohio and what she could do to make sure Andrea and Twinkle were on it.

Kyle didn't return, and soon she heard the phone in her home office ringing. Hugging Muffin to her chest, Dixie ran to answer it. Maybe it was the airline calling to confirm Andrea's flight. Her heart sank when she heard Milo's voice.

"Hi, Dixie. May I please speak to Andrea?"

Dixie leaned out the door to get a glimpse of what was going on upstairs. Andrea was still in the bathroom, and the water in the sink was running.

"She's indisposed," she told Milo.

"Will you tell her I called? I'm planning to ask if she'd like to go to the movies tonight."

"Andrea's supposed to fly back to Columbus, Ohio." Dixie didn't add the *sooner the better.*

"She might change her ticket. We had a good time last night."

"Glad to hear it."

"Yes, Andrea's a real partier," Milo said.

"I gathered."

"In fact, I hope she stays around a while."

"Uh-huh." Muffin was really purring now.

"Have her phone me, okay?" Milo sounded eager, like a little kid.

"Of course, Milo." She made up her mind, *I am definitely going to have to yank the welcome mat out from under Andrea.*

As soon as she hung up, she settled Muffin in the kitchen with a bowl of dry cat food and some water. Then she marched upstairs and rapped on the guest-room door.

"Andrea! I need to talk with you."

"Come in. Do you have Twinkle with you? Where is he, anyway?"

Dixie opened the door to find Andrea lying in bed with the covers pulled up to her chin. "Kyle took Twinkle out. For a walk." Maybe this was true. It *could* be true.

"That's good," Andrea said, closing her eyes. They'd sunk in their sockets, and she was uncommonly pale. The bed, of course, was still not on a frame; mattress and box springs rested on the floor, which meant that Dixie loomed over Andrea. It seemed weird.

"Andrea," Dixie began.

"I'm coming down with a cold."

Dixie let the words register for a long moment. She wondered if there was a chance that Andrea hadn't really spoken them. Andrea may have said, "I think my rummy down is sold," though that didn't make any sense.

"Excuse me?" Dixie said.

"A cold. I probably got it from the people sitting on either side of me on the plane. I was stuck in the middle because all the aisle and window seats were taken. Those guys were coughing and sneezing the whole time."

"Maybe you just had a little too much to drink last night," Dixie said hopefully.

"My throat is on fire and my eyes feel hot. Do you have any cold medicine?"

"Not much," Dixie said. "Wouldn't it be a good idea to get home as soon as you can so you'll be more comfortable?"

If this was ungracious, Andrea apparently didn't notice. "Oh, I can't fly when I've got a cold. It's a bad thing to do. Germs get forced into the eustachian tubes and people go deaf from it. It happened to my friend's mother. Deaf as a post because she flew with a cold."

"I'll see if I can find something," Dixie said, backing out of the room. The last thing she needed to catch was some awful respiratory bug that could lay her up for a week or more.

Kyle was viciously hammering together a birdhouse in the garage when she arrived there.

"Kyle," she said. "We've got a problem."

He stopped hammering. "No, we don't. I tied him to that sawhorse over there." He gestured toward Twinkle, who woofed.

"I don't mean the dog. I'm referring to Andrea. She's sick with a cold. Or at least she says she is. She doesn't want to fly home because germs might rise up her eustachian tubes and make her deaf."

Kyle laid his hammer aside. *"What?"*

"Deaf. Andrea's not flying anywhere for a while, and I don't have it in my heart to make a sick woman leave my house."

"You're too nice, Dixie. I'll talk to her." He started toward the house.

"I suspect she's naked under the blankets," Dixie warned him.

"Trust me, her completely naked body won't do much for me." Kyle kept walking.

"Kyle!"

"Neither would her fully clothed body in case you're worried about it." He turned around, hands on hips.

"Gee, you're cute when you're mad," she said.

"I've heard that before."

"Kyle, if you could—please tell Andrea to call Milo."

"With pleasure," Kyle muttered.

Dixie puttered around in the garage, sweeping up wood chips, pushing aside a bag of fertilizer so she could reach the dustpan. Maybe she should have accompanied Kyle to Andrea's room for this discussion. On the other hand, she trusted him completely. It was just that she would have liked to hear how it was going.

She went back in the house when she ran out of things to do in the garage. She found Kyle sitting at the kitchen table staring moodily into a glass of iced tea. He'd cleaned up the syrup from the floor.

"Well?" Dixie asked.

"She's pretty sick," he said. "I reminded her that it's tax season, and she says she's handling the workload from here, thanks to her laptop and a phone. I suggested that she might be in the way, and she reminded me that you and I are out of the house most of the time due to our jobs. I told her to get out, and she sneezed at me."

"I get the picture," Dixie said as she sank into a chair beside him.

"I'm sorry, Dixie," Kyle said bleakly. "I didn't expect this."

"I'll take her some throat lozenges, the zinc-and-vitamin kind that are supposed to get rid of a cold before it starts."

"Is it possible she's malingering because she's spying on us?"

"She and Milo hit it off big," Dixie informed him. "Maybe she plans to make him fall in love with her."

"By pretending she has a cold? Now, that's a new one."

"Yeah."

"Yeah."

They stared at each other glumly across the kitchen table.

"Kyle? Dixie?" Andrea's voice sounded strained as it wafted weakly down the stairwell.

"What now?" Kyle muttered.

"I'll go," Dixie said, getting up again. "I was going to get her the lozenges anyway."

"No, I will," Kyle said.

"Together," Dixie said, offering her hand, so they climbed the stairs and pushed open Andrea's door.

Their houseguest was pathetic. Her nose was now red, and she was wiping her runny nose. "Do you have any tissues?" she asked Dixie.

"I'll get them." Dixie went to her own bathroom and grabbed a new box of tissues, as well as the lozenges and an unopened squeeze bottle of nasal decongestant.

"Thanks," Andrea said when she reappeared. "I'm sorry about this. I do hope to stay and explore this thing with Milo, but I didn't expect to get sick."

"Huh," said Dixie.

"As soon as you get well, you'll have to leave," Kyle said.

"Where's Twinkle?"

"In the garage, chewing on something," Kyle told her.

Dixie hadn't seen the Yorkie chewing anything, and it occurred to her that Kyle was making this up. She shot him a skeptical glance out of the corner of her eye.

"Could you bring him to me?" Andrea asked plaintively, reaching for the lozenges.

"I'll send him right up," Kyle said. His voice was gruff. He wheeled and stalked out.

"Milo wants you to call him," Dixie blurted before following.

As she rounded the corner into the kitchen, she was met
by a galloping Twinkle. She jumped out of the way in time
to avoid a collision and met Kyle in front of the sink.

"I'm going shopping for a living-room rug," she said,
though she had originally intended to unpack boxes.

"I'm supposed to help a guy build a shoeing stock," Kyle
told her. "He lives between here and Florence." At her blank
look, he said, "A shoeing stock immobilizes a nervous horse
while we put on his shoes."

"Well, that gets us both out of here for the day. See you
around." She slid her arms around his neck and kissed him.

"Tonight. Same place. Be there," he said.

"You got it." She smiled as she headed out the door.

She didn't find a rug, though she did scope out a
department-store sale on bridal gowns. While she didn't have
the nerve to try one on, some of them sure were elegant.

KYLE MET HER in the garage when she arrived home that evening.

"We should move into the playhouse so neither one of us
gets sick," he said.

"There's no TV out there," Dixie objected, closing the car
door after her. "There's no phone, no fax machine, no anything remotely resembling creature comforts."

"Hey," he said, pulling her close. "I got you, babe."

She let herself be hugged for a while. What Kyle said
about avoiding infection made sense, especially since, for her,
staying home from work meant losing a possible sale.

"Have you eaten?" she asked him.

"The guy I was working with offered me some ribs and I took him up on it."

"I grabbed a hamburger at the drive-thru in that new place off I-95. I'm not hungry now."

"So do we move to the playhouse or not?"

"Might as well," she said. She went inside the house, climbed the stairs and listened for Andrea. No sound came from behind the closed guest-room door, so she gathered up clothes and toiletries and left. She and Kyle started down the path to the playhouse with him carrying Muffin and her litter box.

When Kyle set the cat on the floor, Muffin uttered a small inquisitive mew and proceeded to walk around sniffing everything. Dixie and Kyle perched uneasily on the teeny-tiny chairs and contemplated their perplexing situation.

"Maybe Andrea and Twinkle could go to a motel," Dixie suggested. "We could check on vacancies at the Magnolia."

"Any chance she could stay with Milo?" This uttered wishfully.

"He's living with Priss, his sister."

Kyle let out a long exasperated sigh.

"Well. Here we are." She glanced around the playhouse. "The night is still young. It's only six-thirty. What is there to do?"

"I could field a few ideas. Why don't you guess what they are? Hint—there's a reason they call this a playhouse." His grin was happily insinuating.

Dixie ignored it. She was still irked that they hadn't had a chance for that romantic walk under the stars on the night that Andrea had surprised them with her presence. "Maybe this is a good chance to talk about our relationship," she said.

"Hey, do we have to? I'm not Dr. Phil."

"Too bad," she said, disappointed. She had learned how to

close on real estate deals. Why couldn't she close on this thing with Kyle?

He leaned forward earnestly. "Dixie, just because we insert bits and pieces of relationship assessment into other conversations doesn't mean they're invalid." His point made sense.

Maybe this wasn't a good time. She could forgive him for waiting until they could both concentrate on all the heartfelt things that they needed to say to each other, so she leaned over and kissed him. "All right, but if we can't talk about our relationship, we could go visit relatives. That's a very Southern thing to do."

"Some other time." He was eyeing her in that come-hither way that she had learned to like.

"We could continue this discussion in bed," she suggested.

"Someone else beat us to it," he said, angling his head backward. Muffin had curled up in the middle of the cot, the tip of her tail warming her nose.

"Come here," Kyle said, reaching over to caress Dixie's upper arm.

She did. His lap was quite accommodating, and she leaned her forehead against his. They kissed, and Dixie remembered why she was mad about this man. It wasn't his looks or his sense of humor or the way he encouraged her to be the best she could be. It was the way he kissed, as if he really meant it, as if kissing her was the best possible use of his time and effort. As if, as if…as if he loved her?

If only he did. If only he would tell her so. If only they could lie down on the cot and make love until he couldn't stand *not* telling her.

"I think…" she said.

"Don't," he told her, his mouth working its way down her neck. "It's counterproductive."

"I think we should spread blankets on the floor," she said. "So we can be more comfortable."

He kept kissing her until she was so weak that it required superhuman effort to drag the blankets down from a nearby shelf and spread them on the wee section of the floor that wasn't taken up by the chairs, table, cot and Muffin's litter box. Things proceeded from there, but they didn't require talking. Maybe that was better.

On the other hand, wouldn't a good talk clear the air? Or would that only drive Kyle away?

One thing she was sure about, and that was that Kyle was over Andrea. She hoped he'd decide that he'd never be over her, Dixie. And soon.

Chapter Ten

In the morning when Dixie woke up, a heavy ball of fur was sitting on her chest and purring. *Muffin.*

"Kyle?" she said, reaching for him.

Kyle wasn't there.

Her frantic thoughts ranged from *He's gone back to Ohio* to *Maybe I dreamed our wonderful lovemaking of last night* to *What if he went outside to smoke?*

However, Kyle's truck was parked in its usual spot, last night's lovemaking had been better than any dream and Kyle didn't smoke. After a pet-and-purr session, she nudged Muffin off her chest and reclaimed her clothes, which were strewn atop the teeny-tiny chairs. Muffin stretched and headed for the food dish.

"You slut," Dixie told Muffin affectionately, treating her to an extra rub between the ears. "You'll hang out with whoever feeds you."

Which reminded her of Andrea. Which brought her back to Kyle. A glance out the teeny-tiny window revealed Kyle marching toward the playhouse.

"What's going on?" she asked when he came stooping in.

If moving about the playhouse gave her cricks in her neck, she could imagine how difficult it was for him.

"I've been over to the house," he said. "I needed to get clean underwear."

"Speaking of your underwear, how is Andrea today?" She continued yanking up her jeans and reached for her top. She had to bend at the waist before she could get it over her head.

"I'm happy to say that Andrea has nothing to do with my underwear these days. This morning she can hardly talk. I'm going to the drugstore to get her an antiseptic spray for her throat."

Dixie tugged the top down over her midriff.

"Is that really such a good idea, Kyle? Andrea won't have any reason to go as long as you're paying attention to her."

"If she has medicine, she'll get well faster," he said.

"Kyle, it's a well-known fact that you can't cure a cold. All you can do is soothe the symptoms. I say we let her be so uncomfortable that she can't wait to leave."

"I don't agree."

"Then we have an honest difference of opinion." She glared, but he ignored it. Even though she was annoyed with him, she had to admit that last night he'd pulled out all the stops. He was a wonderful lover, considerate and passionate, appreciative and skilled.

Kyle kept talking, as if filling in space with words would calm her misgivings. "I checked with the Magnolia Motel first thing this morning. They don't allow pets. Andrea won't be parted from Twinkle, I'm afraid. I offered to take care of him until she's feeling better, but she won't have it."

"Bad idea, considering that Muffin and Twinkle hate each other," Dixie muttered. She flung the door open and the brisk wind caught it. Gray clouds scudded across the horizon and a mist hung over the lake. The transplanted dogwood trees shimmered in the fog, their leaves pure silver. It had rained again last night, and puddles of water stood in the driveway. Kyle was right behind her as she started toward the house.

"I'm going to get dressed and go to work," Dixie said, flinging the words back over her shoulder. This was *her* house, *her* property, and she couldn't forget that Kyle was responsible for the usurper in their midst. Maybe not directly, but still. However, she couldn't help taking pity on Kyle when they reached the back steps and she slid a surreptitious glance at him. Kyle was clearly a man under duress.

She softened her voice. "What's your plan for the day?"

"I promised I'd walk Twinkle," Kyle said miserably. "Then I'll go to the drugstore."

Dixie nodded and continued into the house. She didn't hear Andrea stirring behind the closed guest-room door, and that was a good thing. She hurried through her shower and makeup, and when she came downstairs, Kyle and Twinkle were in the yard being whipped around by the wind. Twinkle, his hair bow untied, his bangs flopping over his eyes, was wandering in no particular pattern, and it appeared as if the dog were walking Kyle instead of the other way around.

Dixie stuck her head out the back door. "Kyle, I have some toaster pancakes in the freezer. Want a couple?"

"Not right now," he said gruffly. "I'll get something later."

This was okay with her. She was in the mood for a big breakfast at the Eat Right, and besides, Kathy Lou had probably heard all about Andrea's surprise appearance and would be eager for juicy details.

Dixie grabbed her briefcase and hurried outside. Twinkle

was now running around at the end of his leash, maybe hunting for Muffin's trail. There wouldn't be one, since Muffin had never been outdoors, but Dixie wasn't going to bring that up.

She headed for the playhouse.

"Where are you going?" Kyle asked.

"I need to make sure Muffin has enough food and water. No way am I taking her back in the house until Andrea and Attila are gone."

"They'll go. I can promise that."

He didn't say when.

Dixie spent a few minutes petting Muffin, reassuring her that the house would be theirs again soon. Muffin purred and let out a little *Brrup!* as she twined around Dixie's leg. No doubt about it, Dixie was becoming a cat person. Already *was* a cat person.

Kyle and the dog were traversing a grassy strip near the shore as Dixie started for the garage. She paused for a moment, thinking she should walk over to Kyle for their customary goodbye kiss. But he'd turned his back toward her, whether by accident or design she couldn't say, and the grass was wet. She was wearing new suede shoes. Resolutely, she kept walking.

As she backed her car out, Kyle spoke. He was closer now, dragging Twinkle toward the house.

"No treat until you poo-poo," Kyle said.

Dixie braked sharply and stared at him through her open window. "*What* did you say?"

Kyle looked embarrassed. "I was talking to Twinkle."

"Whew. That's a relief." She thought about that missed kiss again, felt a twinge of unhappiness over the whole situation and started to back up.

"Dixie?"

"Yes?"

"I'm really sorry about all this." His expression was so regretful that she didn't doubt his sincerity, but it wasn't enough.

"We'll talk later." She wondered if Kyle remembered that she was planning to call Lana Pillsbry today to find out if she was going to buy that house.

Kyle smiled, forced though it was, and waved. In that moment, Dixie forgot all about their present difficulties. Even though they were going through a rough time, she would spend the whole day missing him. These days she couldn't wait to get home in the evenings because it meant that she and Kyle would be together. Did he know how much she cared about him?

She sure hoped so, or none of this was worth the trouble.

THE EAT RIGHT CAFÉ wasn't so busy that Kathy Lou didn't have time to talk. "I heard she's real pretty," Kathy Lou said as she refilled Ketchup bottles. "And wears expensive clothes."

"Who told you that?" Dixie asked, idly stirring her coffee. Everyone else was sitting at the other end of the counter. This provided a chance for her to chat with Kathy Lou semiprivately.

"Priss. Milo and Andrea stopped by her house on their date."

It was a date? That was news to her, yet it had no real impact. She didn't care what Milo and Andrea did. Right now she'd help them elope if that would make Andrea go away.

"Did Priss say how that went?"

Kathy Lou screwed the top on a bottle and moved to the next one. "I'm not sure. Andrea was pleasant to Priss and the kids. Anyone who can be sweet to Priss's little Howie is okay in my book, seeing as how he never acts friendly. One time Howie nearly ran me down with a shopping cart at Bi-Lo. By the way, Dixie, I heard Lana looked at the Meehan place."

"I hope she buys it," Dixie said fervently, visions of new living-room chairs dancing in her head.

"Ooooh, and speaking of houses, Milo bought a new mobile home to put on that acreage where he's going to start his plant nursery."

"How nice for him." Dixie stood and shelled out a few bills. "I need to get to work."

"Good luck with Lana," Kathy Lou called after her before turning to wait on someone else.

At the office, Dixie tried unsuccessfully to reach Lana. Then she checked with Mayzelle, who was tardy because of a poodle-groomer appointment, and she doodled on her calendar while making follow-up calls on possible listings. It wasn't until late afternoon that she realized she'd started a diary of sorts.

SATURDAY

Plus: Fun day watching Kyle work with horses. Picnic willow tree scribble make love hope for marriage prop???
Minus: Andrea arrive. Twinkle. Sleep on narrow cot. Kyle scribble scribble. Dumb dumb dumb.

SUNDAY

Plus: Church with family. Dinner with family. Visit with Voncille and them. Scribble scribble.
Minus: Andrea still there. Don't get to spend much time with Kyle. Have to sleep on narrow cot. TIRED OF ANDREA!

MONDAY

Plus: Kyle tells Andrea it's over. *Plus plus plus!!!* Get Muffin. Andrea and Milo go off with dogs she stays out all night.☺ Have sex in canoe with Kyle (not Andrea, me).
Minus: Rains hard. No discuss relationship.☹

TUESDAY

Minus: Andrea comes back in a.m. Andrea sick. Sleep on playhouse floor.
Plus: Sleep on playhouse floor with Kyle. No discussion of relationship? maybe plus?? Scribble.

WEDNESDAY

Plus: ?

The phone rang, and when Dixie answered it, she heard Memaw's voice.

"Listen, Dixie Lee, why didn't you tell me about that Ohio woman camping out at your house? I had to hear it from Dottie."

"I've been busy," Dixie said, feeling the start of a headache.

"You can stay with me anytime you like. I'm expecting you tonight without fail, and you won't have to move back home until she's gone."

Dixie had been concentrating so hard on finding ways to get rid of Andrea that she hadn't even considered other options. "Why, thanks, Memaw. Is Kyle welcome, too?"

A long pause. "All right. I like the fellow, even though—"

"Get over it, Memaw. He's moving down here. At least, it seems pretty certain."

"Hallelujah! He's seen the light. Why don't you and Kyle come early enough for supper. I'll open a jar of that pickled okra I made last summer."

Dixie didn't have the heart to remind Memaw that she hadn't actually made the pickled okra, but she assured her that she and Kyle would be there. After they hung up, she headed out to her afternoon appointments with a lighter step because it seemed to her that things were taking a positive turn. Or at least that's what she believed until she returned to the office and found a phone message from Lana Pillsbry saying that she wasn't interested in the Meehan house after all and to have a nice day.

WHEN DIXIE RETURNED HOME, discouraged about all the hard work she'd put into the deal that hadn't gone through, Kyle wasn't there. Andrea was sitting at the kitchen table, spooning up mouthfuls of chicken noodle soup when Dixie entered through the back door. Twinkle was slurping his own little bowl of soup on the floor. He didn't even bark when Dixie walked in. He just kept eating.

"Hi, Dixie," Andrea said, her voice a mere croak. Her hair was straggly and unwashed, her nose red and chapped. She wasn't wearing makeup and her skin color was washed out. Also, her eyes were pale. Dixie wanted to advise her to have eyeliner tattooed on like hers but decided not to mention it because she wasn't sure how Andrea would react.

"I'm glad you're feeling well enough to be up and around," Dixie said. On the way home, she'd made up her mind to seize the bull by the horns. "Mind if we chat?"

"Sure, let's," Andrea replied.

Dixie sat down, germs be hanged. She groped around in her mind for a suitable way to begin the discussion, but Andrea spoke first.

"I'm really sorry about this," Andrea said. "You've been wonderful."

"I'd like to have my house back." A gross understatement, but she'd never believed in overkill.

Andrea shoved her bowl aside. "I told Kyle I can probably leave the day after tomorrow without my eustachian tubes— you know. Didn't he tell you?"

"Something like that." Dixie tried to recall exactly what Kyle had said. She had a lot of things on her mind, the most upsetting of which was Lana's refusal to buy a house that was ideal for her. It was downright depressing, and she was in the mood for a hot bath, a glass of wine and Kyle, though not in that order. She probably wanted Kyle and his easy sense of humor most. He was the only one who was capable of raising her out of the funk she was in.

"Kyle said to tell you he had a horse emergency some-where he hasn't been before. A town called Sumner? Is that right?"

"Sumter. Did he say when he'd be back?"

"No, he didn't. This may be a little presumptuous—"

Since when did that ever stop you?

"—but I believe he's totally in love with you." Andrea seemed resigned.

Dixie took heart from her words. "That's good. I mean, I care about him, too." Another understatement, but she wasn't about to elaborate. This was Kyle's ex-girlfriend she was talking to, for heaven's sake.

Andrea managed a brief smile. She lifted her shoulders and

let them fall. "I'm willing to accept that Kyle and I aren't right for each other. It's sad, but not so sad that I can't move on."

"I'm glad to hear that," Dixie said with the utmost sincerity. She wondered if Andrea was faking the brave smile.

Maybe not, because Andrea's next words indicated that she had another interest. A very peculiar interest, considering the diverse backgrounds of the two people involved.

Andrea leaned forward in her chair. "Dixie, I enjoyed the time I spent with Milo. He, well, he really listened to me."

It's a tough job, but somebody has to do it.

Andrea knotted her forehead. Then she blurted, "Does he like going to the theater?"

Taken by surprise, Dixie was hard put to answer. "I'm not sure. He was in the Yewville Community Theater group when he was a kid." Andrea brightened, so Dixie kept talking. "That tells you that Milo is certainly interested in theater. Why, he played, oh, let me think. A prince, in one play, a raccoon in another. Milo was a great raccoon, positively brilliant." At the risk of sounding like an infomercial, she clamped her mouth shut.

"That's a positive sign. Excuse me for asking your advice, Dixie, but Milo said the two of you were good friends a long time ago."

"It's okay," she said. *I'm going to throw up,* she thought.

"Do you think Milo would come to visit me in Ohio? I'd like him to be my escort for the last community-theater play of the season. I mean, I won't ask him if there isn't a good chance that he'll accept."

"Go for it," Dixie said.

"Oh, Dixie, thanks. You've been such a big help." Andrea beamed, and even though her eyes were watery and her nose resembled something a clown would wear, she was halfway pretty again.

It was time to leave before she and Andrea joined hands and started singing "Kumbayah." She stood up, and Andrea's bathrobe pocket rang.

Andrea extracted her cell phone from its nest of multiple crumpled tissues. She glanced at the caller ID and mouthed the word *Milo* before Dixie fled the room.

When Dixie was on the way out of the house, Andrea, still on the phone, waved a silent goodbye. "Ask Kyle to phone me at my grandmother's," she told Andrea, and Andrea nodded.

Dixie drove to Memaw's through the rapidly falling dusk, wishing she'd been a little more conciliatory with Kyle that morning. It didn't feel right to be on the outs with him. She'd skipped their morning goodbye kiss for the first time ever because she'd been mad at him. Since she'd left that morning, Voncille's words had been scrolling through her mind like the crawl line at the bottom of a TV screen: "Skeeter and I make it a point never to go to bed angry. We always reconcile before we go to sleep."

Dixie was determined to make up with Kyle before bedtime. They'd kiss and hug and reclaim the happiness that always accompanied their being together. It suddenly struck her that this might not be so easy given that there was no chance on God's green earth that the two of them would be sharing a bedroom in her grandmother's house. Still, she could ask.

"OF COURSE I'M *SUPPOSED* to be a prude," Memaw said. Dixie and Memaw were working together in the kitchen cutting up vegetables for stew. "My generation was brought up to be circumspect."

"I gathered," Dixie said, suppressing a wistful sigh and wishing she hadn't posed the question about sleeping with Kyle so bluntly.

Memaw kept talking as if she hadn't heard. "My mother would have been scandalized if I'd so much as suggested that I was sleeping with your grandfather before we were married."

Dixie was certain she hadn't heard correctly. "You were what?"

"Sleeping together," Memaw said blithely, tossing several chunks of celery into the pot. "I haven't told a soul until now. You should be ashamed of yourself, Dixie, for prying it out of me." Memaw's eyes twinkled mischievously.

"I didn't pry!" Dixie protested in amazement, regarding Memaw in a whole new light. "I only asked if you'd mind if Kyle and I did."

"Do you think I haven't figured out what's going on between you two? It's as plain as the noses on your faces that you're madly in love with each other. I'm okay with that, it's just that he's a Yan—"

"Don't say it," Dixie interrupted. "You said you could get over his being a Yankee."

"I'm working on it. Getting back to your grandfather and me. You should have known him in his younger days, Dixie. He was a rake and a scoundrel, leaving broken hearts in his wake like withered stalks in a harvested field. Then he visited my church and our eyes met over our hymnals while the congregation was singing "Amazing Grace." After the service, he asked me if my name was Grace, and I said yes. And he told me that he'd known it all along because I was amazing. Lordy, what a corny thing for him to say, but I sure did love him for it."

"Your name is Frances," Dixie said.

Memaw chuckled. "I lied. Your granddaddy took me for a ride in his car that evening, and soon we were meeting every night. He'd take me to an old tenant cabin on his family farm where he'd set up a bed and kept white lightning in the cupboard."

Dixie was floored. "You and Granddaddy drank *moonshine* together?"

"Oh, sure. His papa made it. The white lightning gave me the courage to go through with my decision to make love with him, and guess what? Your daddy was the result. Everyone said I was a beautiful bride, and nobody said one mean word about your father being born seven months after the wedding. I was twenty-one years old and never regretted not waiting for marriage. You shouldn't, either, sweetie." Memaw clapped the cover on the stew pot and turned down the heat on the burner.

Dixie, still openmouthed in astonishment, followed her grandmother into the living room. "I, um, guess I'll take my things up to the guest room," she stammered, completely unhinged by the tale she'd been told.

"Go right ahead. Oh, here comes Bubba, and he's brought somebody with him. It's been a while since I've seen that boy. He used to drop in all the time to say hello and find out if I'd baked anything lately, and now I hear he and his wife are expecting a young one. People do get married and have children later these days. Must be because everyone uses those condiments."

"You mean condoms," Dixie said, suppressing a giggle.

"Condoms. I hope you and Kyle do."

"Mmm," Dixie said. She wasn't about to discuss this with Memaw.

At the top of the stairs, Dixie turned for one last perplexed glance at her grandmother. Memaw Frances was as cool as they come, fluffing her perfectly coiffed white hair and straightening her apron before she greeted her guests.

Dixie continued into the guest room, closed the door and indulged in one good long bout of silent, hysterical laughter. When she finished, tears were streaming down her cheeks and she had to splash her face with cool water before she could welcome Bubba.

Her own grandmother a wild young woman? Drinking moonshine and sneaking around to indulge in illicit sex? It was almost more than a body could stand.

AS TWILIGHT SETTLED IN, Kyle drove home from Sumter with the morning's disagreement with Dixie fresh in his mind. Worst of all, he believed everything was his fault. Maybe that wasn't fair. Andrea hadn't caught a cold on purpose, and she seemed okay about their breakup now. When he'd brought her the throat spray, she'd interrogated him relentlessly about Milo. Kyle had stated that he really didn't know the guy, but if Dixie liked him, that meant he was okay.

He had little patience for Andrea's grilling when he was concerned about the way things were going with Dixie. He realized that he should have apologized to her for his abruptness that morning before she went to work. He should have made sure they kissed goodbye. She wasn't exactly angry with him. But she was miffed. Upset. And life was too short to let that sort of thing interfere with their lives.

Hell, they'd never even discussed their relationship except in, well, *excerpts*. Dixie had made it clear that this rankled, and such a talk was overdue. Now he resolved to initiate it.

Maybe it was even time to spring for the engagement ring. He liked the idea of watching it sparkle on her finger, and he grinned to himself. He enjoyed making her happy.

His mind ranged over the past few weeks, yearning for the warm aura of acceptance surrounding Dixie and wanting her certainty and contentment. Dixie's relatives were always lively, sometimes amusing and a real treat for someone who had no extended family whatsoever. By now he couldn't imagine living in a house that didn't contain Dixie. When he was away from her, it was as if an important part of him was missing. All day, knowing that she wasn't in a good mood, he'd felt as if something had been gnawing on his heart. Like Twinkle chewing his pants legs or his shoes, which the Yorkie had savaged more than once.

Kyle didn't like that feeling at all. He preferred the pleasure of coming home to Dixie and being welcomed with open arms. He cherished their nights in bed when they turned to each other in the dark and held each other tight, and he was captivated by how she sometimes murmured his name in her sleep. She was the strong independent woman he'd always wanted, but she made it clear that she depended on him, as well. He appreciated her cooking and her ambition, and he admired her churchgoing habits. His life since he'd met her had been filled with kisses, with laughter, with lovemaking. They'd built something warm and solid between them. He had grown as a result of knowing her, and he never cared to go back to the emptiness of his old life. For his own sake, he needed to tell Dixie all of that. Soon.

He punched the radio tuner to WYEW and listened idly to Kenny Rogers singing "Have I Told You Lately That I Love You?" A few sprinkles from the sky turned into a steady rainfall, and he switched on the windshield wipers. Their steady swish seemed to speak the name that had become so dear… *Dix-ie, Dix-ie, Dix-ie.* She was the most important person in his life now, maybe for all time.

The song on the radio ended, and the deejay cleared his throat. He proceeded to read a news flash.

"The county sheriff's office has issued a bulletin about an accident on the Allentown Road near Lyndale Crossroads. All drivers are urged to avoid the intersection due to a collision that has blocked the passage of vehicles until the road can be cleared." There was more, but Kyle didn't hear it.

He was driving on the Allentown Road, and if his memory was correct, the highway crossing it up ahead was in the small hamlet called Lyndale. He might be approaching that accident, and he'd needed to find an alternate route. He recalled a narrow cutoff that followed a power-line easement, and he believed it circled around and reentered the Allentown Road not far from Dixie's grandmother's house.

Sure enough, as he rounded the curve, he spotted the Day-Glo vest of a deputy who was redirecting traffic at an intersection. There was one truck ahead of him, and it was full of unsettled chickens on their way to market. He was paying more attention to the plight of the chickens than to the accident, the view of which was blocked by the trunks of several big trees.

The deputy, looking at his truck, signaled him to pull over. Kyle rolled down his window.

"You the coroner?" the deputy asked.

His truck had been mistaken for a coroner's van before. "No, I'm not." He gestured toward the wreck. "How's it going?"

The deputy, a dour, long-faced fellow, shook his head.

"It's a bad one. A tanker truck skidded on the curve and hit a convertible."

"Survivors?"

The deputy shrugged. "Can't say. Detour to your left, please."

Kyle swiveled his head in the direction of the accident as he made the turn. All he saw was a mangled mass of debris. He couldn't make out shapes, but then maybe there weren't any left. The scene was illuminated by flashing red and blue emergency lights and the shouts of rescue workers. He spared a thought for the accident victims' loved ones who would be waiting at home unaware that wives or husbands or children wouldn't be there for dinner.

The road looped back around, and suddenly the only thing between him and the accident scene was a wide fenced field. He was too far away to register many particulars, but he was able to make out the tanker lying on its side and the blue car it had hit. The car was crushed, the engine rammed back into the passenger compartment. He braked and scanned the scene.

An ambulance was driving away from the wreck, traveling slowly as if in no particular hurry. That was bad. If a survivor were riding in the ambulance, it would be rushing to the hospital.

The car. A blue car, and the blue the exact shade of Dixie's Mustang. The deputy had said the car was a convertible. His heart quickened, and he could scarcely breathe. Despite her penchant for fast driving, he wouldn't let himself believe that it could be Dixie. He racked his brains trying to remember what she was going to do that day. She'd mentioned appointments, she said she was going to the Eat Right for breakfast, and by now she'd be home.

Or *would* she be at home with Andrea staked out there? The house Dixie hoped to sell Lana was located off the Allentown Road, so she could have had a reason to go there today, especially late in the afternoon when Lana would have left work and might insist on taking another look.

He speeded up. If he could find an alternate route leading back to the Allentown Road, maybe approaching from the opposite direction, he'd be able to check and make sure that Dixie wasn't involved. His heart in his throat, he dialed her cellphone number. She didn't answer, and his palms began to sweat. Dixie always kept her phone nearby in case she received a business call. She was hardly ever without it. Oh, if it was Dixie in that accident, he'd never forgive himself for that morning.

Sometimes when you're threatened with losing someone you love, you begin to see things with crystal clarity. You realize where you went wrong and what you should have done instead. Kyle felt everything tumbling in on him, and the very things about their relationship that he had contemplated only a few moments ago became monumental in importance. All the things he should have done, that he should have said, and what if he never had the chance? What if he lost Dixie, the most precious human being in the world? What if he never got to buy her that engagement ring?

Frantic by now, fighting the sharp bite of nausea in his gut, he slowed to assess an unpaved road on his right, but it turned out to be a driveway. It wouldn't take him back to the accident scene, so he kept going, exceeding the speed limit now, unable to worry about the slick highway or the many curves or his own well-being. He needed to know Dixie was safe.

Now he was in familiar territory. He passed the turnoff to

the lake, and coming up was a familiar roadside sign touting nematocides. Beyond that, Memaw Frances's house nestled into the tree-dotted landscape, but he wouldn't stop there. He needed to get home. He needed Dixie.

At Frances's house, a number of cars were parked out front. He braked sharply as he noticed Bubba's truck. Another car he didn't recognize was there, and on the other side of it was a blue one. A Mustang convertible.

Relief washed over him at the sight of that car. His knees went weak even as his brain grappled with the reality that Dixie was at her memaw's, not in an ambulance. He parked behind Bubba's pickup, where he sat for a long moment and got a grip on himself. When he was ready to open the car door, another worry surfaced. What if something had happened to Frances?

He ran to the front door, hammered on it. By the time someone flung it open, he was ready to burst inside uninvited.

"Why, Kyle," said Frances, beaming up at him affectionately. "Come in and join us."

"Is Dixie—?" he stammered, needing to set eyes on her for himself. Because she might not be here, never mind her car out front. It was just a heap of metal and plastic and miscellaneous parts, not a person, and people were the most important thing in the world when they were *your* people. And she was his, he had always known it, and he should have taken steps to make her permanently his long before this.

"Kyle?" Dixie said, and her voice with its Southern lilt was as sweet as the scent of spring flowers borne on a freshening breeze.

She descended the stairs, and the sight of her made his heart leap in his chest. Once he would have disallowed anyone's claim that merely setting eyes on someone could cause such an effect. Once he had considered such notions romantic frippery. But now—now he had Dixie.

She walked to the door as if this was any ordinary day and presented her cheek for his kiss. In that moment, Bubba faded away, and Chad, whom he belatedly noticed leaning against the mantel, and Frances and her friend Dottie, whose car that must be beside Dixie's. For Kyle, no one else existed, and he drew a deep breath and closed his eyes for a long moment of thanksgiving before enfolding Dixie in his arms.

He held her close, the pulse in her temple beating against his cheek, the fragrance of her hair in his nostrils. And he couldn't wait one more instant to tell her how he felt.

He pulled slightly apart so that he could watch her facial expression. He took a deep breath and let the words tumble out.

"Dixie, I love you. I should have told you long ago, and—and I don't understand why I didn't. But if you'll have me, I want to marry you." His eyes searched the depths of hers, one small part of him afraid that she wouldn't accept. They'd known each other a comparatively short time. But if he was so certain in his own mind that this was the way it should be, surely Dixie was, too.

At first her lovely face registered bewilderment, which gave way to confusion, and his heart almost stopped. Then, at long last, there was joy.

He'd never forget the exquisite happiness in her voice in that moment. "Oh, Kyle. Of course I'll marry you."

"Do you love me?" *First things first.* He should have found that out before he'd impetuously blurted his proposal, but it wasn't as though his thoughts were arriving sequentially right now.

She blinked. "I love you more than I can say." Though some of the words came out strangled with emotion, they were what he'd hoped to hear.

He kissed her then, not once but twice, then three times. She threw her arms around his neck and kissed him back in a decidedly lustful manner. That must be what started the hoots and hollers from Bubba and Chad.

Brought back to reality by their commotion, he stopped kissing Dixie. Believe it or not, he'd forgotten that there were any people in the room but the two of them.

Bubba applauded, and Chad joined in. Frances said, "I do declare!" Her friend Dottie appeared nonplussed.

Chad grinned approvingly. "I give you credit, bro. That's the best marriage proposal I've ever heard in my life. Not that I've heard all that many."

"Me, too," said Dottie in a quavering voice. She was an elderly woman wearing too much blusher, or maybe she was just embarrassed by the wild display of emotion on his part.

Frances didn't miss a beat. "Welcome to the family," she said. "Even though you are a Yan—"

"Memaw," warned Dixie, and Frances bit her lip.

Kyle knew what Frances had been about to say, but she was easy to forgive. "For your information, Frances," he said, still hanging on to Dixie for dear life, "I'm planning to switch sides. Chad has invited me to join his group of Confederate reenactors."

"You did?" Dixie asked Chad.

Chad shrugged. "Why not."

"And you'll try it?" she asked Kyle.

"If they don't mind a Yankee in their midst."

"Yeehaw!" Chad shouted, a full-blown rebel yell.